THE SLIGHTLY ALTERED

HISTORY OF CASCADIA

A Fantasy for Grown Ups

Linda B. Myers

Earl –
To friendship!

Linda B Myers

About This Book

The Slightly Altered History of Cascadia is a work of fiction. Names, characters, places and happenings are from the author's imagination. Any resemblance to actual persons – living or dead – events or locales is entirely coincidental.

No part of this book may be used without written permission, except in the case of brief quotations in critical articles and reviews. Email inquiries to myerslindab@gmail.com

Published 2017 by Mycomm One
© 2017 by Linda B. Myers
ISBN: 978-0-9986747-3-5
Cover design by introstudio.me
Interior design by Heidi Hansen

For updates, news, blog and chatter:
www.LindaBMyers.com
Facebook.com/lindabmyers.author
www.amazon.com/author/lindabmyers
myerslindab@gmail.com

Dedication

To every spirit and human, horse and bear
who fights the good fight

PART ONE

Wherein the gods admit to a blunder
in the creation of humans
and the spirit Cascadia comes to be

CHAPTER ONE

Before recorded time, First Female and Old Man Above coaxed life from the brilliance of the stars and reflective glory of the moon. Of all their earthly places, they most loved the forests, ocean, and mountains of Cascadia. Now this paradise was threatened by a phenomenon inexplicable to the two gods: the human rage that was destroying the globe had entered their beloved wilderness. It must be stopped.

"Humans are imperfect fabrications, often nasty as wolverines even when their bellies are full. They are angry with each other in ways that mystify every Presence here, phantasm and deity alike. You must have missed an essential lyric in their Creation Song. Do something," First Female demanded.

Old Man Above heard it as nagging. If she said it once, she'd say it ... well, she'd probably say it again. The truth was that he was disappointed in their human creations, too. Wearily he rousted himself from his splendid view of the Northern Lights, reached far below and drew up a dripping ball of odiferous muck. "Here," he said, handing the mess to First Female. "Let's just see what you can do."

She looked at the hunk of ooze and smiled. "I'll create a spirit, I think, one who looks human enough to walk among them and correct the errors in their construction. Oh, not a survival of the fittest type, slashing and burning. I will use a more feminine concept. This creation will listen before she acts. She'll observe before she obliterates.

"I will provide her a way to soar across Cascadia, length to breadth, mountain to shore, so she may detect and fix human foibles. And I will even give her invisibility on demand. Invisibility has worked well for us all these eons."

Old Man Above merely grunted and turned his attention back to the light game streaking color across the sky.

First Female decided to name her creation Cascadia to honor the region, knowing that a spirit so named would be one with the earth, the sea and the sky. "The name has beauty in its sibilance, a softness that will mask the steel this spirit must possess to assess the rage around her."

"Whatever," said Old Man Above.

First Female called to the gods and goddesses in the Chamber of Mythologies. She explained they would be asked to teach *emotional* skills which the newly minted Cascadia would need to walk among the humans. Next, First Female visited the Tree of Human History. There, she selected *physical* Skill Masters.

Her planning complete, First Female sang her Creation Song, and Cascadia came to be.

* * *

This was not the first assault Cascadia had observed since First Female sent her on her way all those weeks before. The spirit watched the human

3

male from the high boughs of a cedar tree that surrounded her like a living cave. If he looked her way, he would see nothing but a pattern of greenery and blue sky. Cascadia and her flying bear were invisible.

She could tell this particular human was not at home in the forest. He appeared ill-equipped and untrained. He acted lost, requesting directions home from the human girl who was picking wild chanterelles, her bag heavy with the earthy crop.

When he spoke to her, the brown-skinned girl smiled at him. Then she turned her golden eyes away long enough to point the way out of the forest. Cascadia had seen this sort of kindness in humans before. But the man grabbed the girl, tied her hands with her own sash, bent her over a fallen hemlock tree and took her. Afterwards, he used the machete.

"He is killing her," Cascadia muttered to the great bear beside her, speaking no louder than a slight breeze in the forest. "Does he not recognize her pain?" Blood from the broken body of the savaged girl dampened the yellow lady slippers and Indian paint brush. The animals of the forest would soon discover the carrion, and the man would survive to kill another day. He was cleaning blood from his machete when he tensed, stared all around as well as high above.

Does he hear more than the wind moaning in the trees? Does he see my shadow? Does he feel any sense of doom?

Cascadia could only question. She was under orders to observe not intervene. No matter how much it rankled, she was to stay out of conflict for now. First Female had commanded it weeks before in a melodic

4

utterance that swirled around the spirit. The voice had no visible origin. It just *was*, imposing and undeniable. Cascadia obeyed.

Silver Tip, the flying bear, scented the fresh blood and grew restive. The spirit climbed onto his back, then evaporated with him into the mist and flew away through the trees. She traveled on, memorizing every hollow, lake and glacial ridge of Cascadia, the region for which she was named.

Over time, Cascadia had discovered that one earth species often killed another to live, but only humans maimed their own kind for sport. She had no concept of why. She could feel basic emotions in the same way as the forest mammals around her. Like them, she experienced fear, joy and shame. She just didn't know these feelings by name or how to control them as they came and went.

Cascadia clung to Silver Tip, putting her arms around his massive neck, burrowing into his fur. She'd grown used to travelling at wind speed on the back of her ursine steed. The freedom was intoxicating.

But her liberty was about to end.

* * *

Helen of Troy appeared one day and changed everything.

Cascadia was playing in the chill water of a swift-moving creek, right where it bent back on itself to create a quiet pool. She'd splashed Silver Tip as he tried to land yet another salmon. Believing they were alone she didn't bother with the wrap of invisibility which required much of her energy when in use. She was taken by surprise when a husky voice spoke to her.

"I've been sent by First Female," it announced. "Take it from me, honey, it's your good fortune she chose me considering some of the nut jobs in the Chamber of Mythologies. Like that crazy damn Cyclops. But don't get me started."

Cascadia began to fade, literally.

"Oh, quit with the disappearing act. I can see you anyway, what with not being human and all." The goddess, holding a rolled golden scroll in one elegant hand, flounced down on a riverbank boulder, crossed her long legs and rested the other hand on her knee. A gold and opal ring spanned her index finger knuckle to knuckle. Cascadia had never seen anything like it. She'd never seen breasts that size, either.

"I'm called the Goddess of Lust. That makes me quite a different kettle of fish from those namby-pamby Vestal Virgins. My earthly form was Helen of Troy, the most delectable woman of all time. As you can see. You may call me Helen or Goddess, as you wish. Come out of the water now. Sit and listen. You won't believe what you are about to hear."

Silver Tip bounded forward in one bearish leap. His vaults terrified everyone and everything. But this goddess stopped him with a languid wave of her hand. "Quiet you," she snapped. "Lay down."

He lifted his lip to assert his considerable authority. But her voice cut off his roar before it could rumble free of his vocal chords. "You're nothing but an oversized hairball. Damned smelly one, at that."

The crestfallen bear lowered himself to the ground with a resounding juicy fart.

"How rude," the goddess muttered, fanning her hand in front of her face with urgency. "That would not be allowed on Mount Olympus. Standards are certainly low in this goddess-forsaken wilderness."

Cascadia rose from the creek, water plastering her thin clothes against her slender form. She was not used to being seen, much less stared at in the way the Goddess of Lust was watching her now. She felt heat spread from her neck to her cheeks but knew no word for a blush.

"What on earth are you wearing?" Helen asked.

"My uniform is called shorts and a t-shirt. They were given to me by First Female as typical of human apparel. To wear when I am visible."

"What's that marking on the shirt?" Helen peered at it.

Cascadia looked down at the pattern which was damp and distorted now as it rose and fell over her twin peaks. "I do not know. Some kind of hieroglyphic that humans wear. I have other such shirts with other such writings. But I do not read the language."

"I doubt First Female does either, her fashion sense being what it is. Ah, well. We'll work on wardrobe. For now, spin around and let me see all your angles."

Cascadia did as ordered. If First Female had sent this goddess from the Chamber of Mythologies, then there must be a good reason. *Who am I to question?* Nevertheless, Cascadia questioned all the while.

Helen tapped a manicured finger against her full pursed lips. Then she unrolled her scroll and stared at it. By stretching as she turned and peeking downward, Cascadia could just see the buxom females sketched on the papyrus.

"All righty then," Helen said at last, rolling the scroll shut. "You may stop spinning. You are more of a reed than the beauties of my day. A craft project in much need of improvement. But you are workable clay. With my help you will be unequalled in beauty among humans today."

"Why would I want that?" Cascadia asked feeling just the slightest bit dizzy from spinning. Or maybe from Helen. She lowered herself next to Silver Tip, sitting on the forest floor which was blanketed with soft fir needles, ferns and mosses. She could feel the silent growl vibrating in the bear's body, telling her he did not like this troublesome goddess.

"Because, darling, lust moves men." Helen raised both her brows and rolled her eyes in a 'duh' sort of way. "And beauty is a part of lust."

Cascadia exchanged a shrug with Silver Tip then said, "I want to move men?"

"Well, of course! Of course you do. And there's no better way than lust. Especially, if you want to have a bit of fun along the way for yourself. But," and here Helen pointed a finger with all the weightiness of a gun. "It must be in your control, not theirs."

Cascadia experienced bewilderment although she didn't know the word nor did she like the feeling. *In my control? What does this goddess mean? What on earth was First Female thinking, sending her to me?* She stared at the goddess with concentration.

Helen of Troy appeared human but more so. Enhanced. Her voice was huskier, her skin more aglow, her lips a poutier bow. She was spectacular, with laugh lines around her mouth and wisdom in her eyes, eyes the exact color of the first wild irises in the spring. Cascadia could see her body through the thin silk, backlit by the setting sun. It was plusher than the spirit's own build, round and luscious.

"What is this covering that you have?" Cascadia asked. It was quite different from her own attire.

The goddess explained it was a Greek chiton, very lust friendly ... merely two squares of material sewn up the sides, belted with a golden sash below her breasts. It was toga-like, made of silk as light as a butterfly wing. The ornamental brooches holding her gown at the shoulders were golden cats whose tails formed the clasps. "So easy to undo," Helen said with a slow bat of lengthy eyelashes. A braid that matched the sash twisted its way up her arm, and a golden filament net captured her raven curls on the top of her head.

To the lithe, athletic Cascadia, Helen of Troy's softness cradled in the diaphanous get-up was as distinct from her own form and wardrobe as a third sex. How was she to arouse any of this emotion that Helen called lust?

"First Female sang the Creation Song in order to craft you," Helen said. "That much you already know. You have been honored with a mission that is very dear to her. To help you succeed, you have been given humanoid shape, invisibility on demand and, goddess help you, a flying bear. You are to scrutinize the savagery that is poisoning this land today and, if possible, learn how to fix it. First Female and Old Man Above believe there is still hope for the world or they would have never made you the namesake for this part of it."

Helen made the rocking motion with one hand that is the universal gesture for maybe so, maybe not. "I don't get the attraction to this place, myself. I mean, it's pretty enough but far too damp and chill for my tastes. Where is the sun and the desert sand? And what do you do at night other than shiver? Where are the brave warriors, the feasts, the orgies? Now, Mount Olympus, that was one rocking mountain. But I digress. I must teach you the skill of lust, and it will take some preparation. Tell me, do you have figs, pistachios or orchid bulbs to nibble on?"

Cascadia had never heard of these things.

"Never mind." Helen fiddled with a lustrous curl that had escaped the golden net. "I'll get you some. They're aphrodisiacs, you know. One day you'll learn the Skills of the Flora from another tutor." She leaned forward to say in a whisper, "Of course, compared to me that Celtic herbalist is a pagan pig so you be careful around him if he ever appears with his nasty bag of tricks."

She stood, lightly brushing her own cheek with one long finger. "You've perhaps noticed that I am exquisite."

Cascadia nodded. Silver Tip rumbled a protest but she quieted him with a touch to his ear.

"Oh, since my teens, I may have gained a pound or two. Having many children will do that to you, and the little snots are never really grateful for your sacrifice." The goddess spied a fawn lily so well hidden amongst the boulders that Silver Tip had not eaten it. She plucked the speckled white bloom and put it in her hair.

"Now where was I? Oh, yes. Lust. Today's lesson is about what lust *is*. So let's begin with the good and the bad of it." She seated herself gracefully back on her boulder. "All through time, a human woman's greatest weapon against men has been her ability to turn their silly heads. We make their eyes bulge and their jaws drop. The vagina is arguably the most valuable article on earth. Its worth exceeds gold. It has started more battles than religion.

"I hasten to add that this possession has its downside. Take my mother, Nemesis, for instance. She wanted nothing to do with my father, Zeus, so she changed herself into a goose. Of course, he changed himself into a gander, and you can guess what happened next. I tell you, it's embarrassing to be born of an egg."

"Born of an egg?" Cascadia whispered into Silver Tip's ear. He huffed, his enormous nose twitching. She felt her lips part and a sound like the gurgle of a brook passed through. She'd made the noise before but didn't know what it was, just that she liked it.

"Sure, go ahead and laugh. You, too, you wretched excuse for a fur rug," Helen snapped at them both. "But just think. If an unattractive sort of presence like Mom can make a man turn himself into a large bird, imagine what a really special female can do. Like me. That bit about launching a thousand ships? It's true. I've been kidnapped twice, married a king, taken a lover, taken my lover's brother, and my lover's other brother. Then all I had to do to get the Mister back was drop my chiton before his eyes. He instantly forgave my little misadventures as part of a youthful spirit. And I've lived, as they say, happily ever after ever since."

The look of triumph on Helen's face was quickly replaced with caution. "But beware, kiddo. In the Chamber of Mythologies, there are more gods and demons and phantasms representing shades of lust than any other emotion. At the gentle end of the spectrum you have Dogoda, the Slavic spirit of the West Wind. The blush in your cheeks reveals that you've already known his tender touch."

Cascadia was found out. She'd met Dogoda and eagerly awaited his return. She sought him along the creeks and edges of the forest. When the caressing wind had first arrived, he'd carried her with the leaves, swirling and dancing in the air. His warm, moist breath made her tremble and tumble, her legs and arms and mouth open wide to catch him wherever, however she could. The life force of him lifted her, enthralling her with his sweet sadness and his faithful promise of return. She'd drifted in his arms, and then he was gone until the seasons would return him to her once more next autumn.

So that is lust. I begin to understand.

It was a mystery solved, a poem deciphered. Cascadia now had a word for the delightful feeling.

The wisdom of Helen escalated in her eyes. First Female was right again.

Helen's grim tone brought her back from ecstasy. "You must learn this, Cascadia: lust can take on darker forms. Mythic gods around the earth can be devastatingly cruel. I myself was raped twice as a child. Satyrs hunt down unsuspecting women. Succubi ravish men in the night until they die. The Moroccan Qandisa seduces youngsters in order to drive them insane."

Cascadia was more than a little baffled. Maybe lust wasn't so delightful after all, not if it could lead to lunacy.

"Lust is an itch, a craving. Inextinguishable desire. Whether it is reviled or adored by humans, considered a sin or rapture, well, that depends on which of the gods they worship in the Chamber of Mythologies."

Cascadia thought back to the brown-skinned girl in the woods, murdered by the human male after their brutal coupling. "It is dangerous for humans, this emotion that can feel so good or hurt so bad." She saw how volatile lust could be. It was not to be trifled with.

"Yes. You must *control* the men who want you. You cannot be in their power."

"But how will I overpower them?"

"When you're ready, I'll bring you a human who is the Skill Master of the Knife. First Female has selected him as your teacher." Helen cocked her head and winked. "I think he can teach you a thing or two about lust, as well."

* * *

The following morning Cascadia and Silver Tip, asleep in the swaying branches of a cedar tree, were awakened by an eerie song. Was it a bird that could harmonize with itself? It was so strange, so beautiful, so foreign to Cascadia, both the spirit and the region alike.

Then a familiar sound joined in. A rapid rat-a-tat deep in the forest stopped and an ear-splitting caw began.

"Hammer!" Cascadia cried as loud as she could. "Hammer, come!"

In a flurry of shiny black plumage, the pileated woodpecker landed in the boughs above Cascadia and Silver Tip. The elegant bird was big as a crow, decorated with a bright red crest and white stripes from his cheeks down his neck. His raucous voice made him the messenger of the forest.

"Hammer, what is this new song? Is it a bird I don't yet know?"

The bird shrieked a maniacal laugh.

"Yes. That's the sound. New to you, too? Then we will investigate. First Female be with you, Hammer."

Off he flew. Soon the distant rat-a-tat began again as Hammer resumed feasting on insects burrowing in the trees.

The spirit and her bear followed the unknown song back to the forest pool they had visited the day before. Enough sunlight filtered through the trees to warm Cascadia's body and lighten Silver Tip's dour morning mood.

14

At the pool, there was no living bird. Instead, Helen of Troy was creating the musical resonance on something that looked like pieces of reeds. The goddess stopped and said, "It's called a syrinx after one of the nymphs that Pan pursued. I stole it from him while he was teaching the shepherd boys to pleasure themselves."

Cascadia didn't know what that meant, and Helen didn't explain. The goddess tucked the multi-piped flute into an ivory box perched on a boulder beside her. The box looked smaller than the flute to Cascadia but she must have been seeing things.

How can a shell be smaller than the nut inside?

Helen next extracted a mysterious tool from the box and held it out to the spirit. It was a round circle about the size of Silver Tip's forepaw. One side had a golden carving of a naked man riding a ram. The other side was polished smooth to an extreme shine.

"This is a reflecting glass," Helen explained as Cascadia took it from her hand. "You can see yourself in it. Take a look."

I can already see myself by looking down at my body. That's how Cascadia knew she was human in shape and bronze as the tribes like the Molala, S'Klallam, and Nootka. But she'd never seen her own face other than in the rippling water on the forest pool. She eagerly looked into the marvelous glass and saw a human face looking back. It wasn't wrong exactly, neither was it right. It was like an unfinished drawing of a face. She was certainly no Helen, and she observed with some dismay, "I am … I am … plain."

15

Helen agreed. "Yes, my little honey cake, you are."

Cascadia was alarmed by her reflection's lack of ... *essence.* She had observed enough humans to know she was not unique in any way. Her eyes were okay but only okay. Her cheekbones were high but not too high. She had no expression whatsoever. There were none of the character lines like those in the faces of the human women she had seen. No dimples like those of Helen, no sparkle in her eyes, no laugh lines, no freckles. Nothing but an empty expanse, a field left fallow.

"But there is reason for such plainness," Helen said. "First Female gave you the form of an adult female human, but with none of the depth or the experience. No *je ne sais quoi* as those bitchy French goddesses would say."

"I am dull," Cascadia said with a sigh. Silver Tip rubbed his head against her, perhaps offering the comfort of a human's companion animal. But it nearly knocked her over.

"Quit with the complaints," Helen of Troy snapped. "No reason to despair. In time you will feel all that humans feel, taught to you by goddesses and human ancients and soon, a human familiar. Your visage will reflect all that you know. You shall earn essence on your own." She took the mirror from Cascadia to place it back in the ivory box just as Silver Tip moved forward to see himself as well. Helen flicked him on an ear with scroll she held. "Be gone, Badness of Bear. This lesson does not concern you."

The grizzly whined his irritation. He'd let Cascadia know he wanted to bite this pushy sow of a goddess into two chewy morsels. But there'd be hell to pay from Old Man Above and First Female. He thought of them as *They Who Command All Living Things Even Those with Fearsome Might.*

Silver Tip had been born one of their Chosen Ones, allowed to grow free and wily all his days on earth. Of course, First Female had extracted payment for this forbearance. Gods don't allow long and mellow lives without recompense, not even to the biggest bear in the woods. His new job was to watch over Cascadia. He had agreed to be her obedient steed, so First Female had given him the gift of flight to make him greater than all other bears.

He figured he'd already been pretty great. Little in the forest was a danger to him while he picked berries or uplifted rotting logs to find the fat tasty grubs underneath. He was inherently a peace-loving soul. But now this ... this ... she-monster was crawling up his ass all the time. Worse yet, Cascadia accepted Helen, so he had to put up with her. As requested he ambled away. Maybe he'd pester the fish in the creek and then scratch his back on that Douglas fir stump that was even broader than his own considerable width.

When he had gone, Helen turned her attention to the contents of her ivory box. "I have a gift for you to add to those you've already received from First Female. I've never shared this with a spirit and certainly not with a human. It's too dangerous for them to muck about with it. Besides, it's *my* recipe,

17

and I suck at sharing. Wouldn't share it with you if First Female hadn't threatened me with cellulite." As she spoke, Helen extracted tiny clay pots and emptied a little bit of this plus a dash of that into a chalice made from entwined grapevines. "A snippet of sex, sprinkle of power potion, teaspoon of knowledge, pinch of passion." As she poured in one element after another, she swirled the chalice ever so gently. The cup began to radiate a ruby glow, then burst into a rainbow aura that surrounded Cascadia. She felt its warmth head to toe.

"Add stardust and fairy flirtation and floral lips from Georgia O'Keefe. Top off with a touch of velvet, the feel of satin, moist and warm." The brilliantly hued glow that surrounded Cascadia was suddenly perfumed with blossoms and spices and musk.

"Okay, that's done. Be thankful I don't mess about with frog toes and dog tongues." Helen held the chalice up before the spirit's eyes.

"Do I drink it now?"

"Good goddess, no! What gave you that idea? You merely whiff it in."

Cascadia sniffed once and then inhaled with greater force. Miraculously, the rainbow disappeared with a tingling inside her nostrils. She'd drawn all the colors of the elixir into her body. The warmth she'd felt outside now heated all her bits and pieces within. She gasped in pleasure.

"This is my secret," said Helen. "The reason all men worship me is that I look different to each of them. A man sees in me his favorite fantasy female. And now the same is true of you."

18

Cascadia was alarmed. "They will all want to lust with me?" It seemed rather a lot to ask of her. As yet, she saw no reason to be interested in human men.

"It will often be so. But remember, desire differs man to man. For some, a favorite fantasy may be for unassailable purity. Or a love lost decades ago. Or even a sweet longing for a daughter to raise and protect."

"If each man sees me as a different vision, how will I keep it all straight?"

"You are in control, remember? You will not be affected by those who do not interest you. Those burning colors now within your core will sear others who come too near unbidden. It is only the man you chose whose fantasy you will see. It is his fantasy that you will become in look, action and attitude. The other men's desires mean nothing to you."

"What about you? Will you see me in this fantasy world?"

"Yes, because it is my elixir. And I am your teacher."

"What about a human woman? What will she see?"

"When you choose to appear, she will see you as you really are, in one of those ghastly t-shirts and absurd pants. Why First Female wouldn't have at least chosen a little black dress, I have no clue. Any more questions?"

Cascadia's brain was so full at the moment there was no room for another thought. She sat quietly, assimilating all she'd heard. "When men look at me they will see their favorite fantasy. I will see and be the fantasy of the man I chose. Women will see me as me unless I wear invisibility.

"Okay, then. We'll move on. First Female has selected a familiar for you. A person for you to trust, one that understands the quirks that make humans tick because she *is* one. None of us gods can do that."

"Who is she?"

"Her name is Shaylee Ward."

CHAPTER TWO

Blue was a bad boy, so of course Shaylee loved him. "Two thousand pounds of juvenile delinquent," she'd been known to mutter in his ear.

He was the sole gelding and only member of the team still under four years of age. Blue was more interested in plucking thistles from their spiny stems with his delicate lips than in having a snaffle bit wedged between them. He got a charge out of head butting the boss lady in the back if she wasn't quick about getting the horse collar around his massive neck.

The rest of the team today was comprised of three no-nonsense mares who knew the drill. Violet was the juvie's mother, and a distinctive blue roan just like him. The other mares, Gracie and Gabrielle, were the dappled gray more common to the Percheron breed. Each was 18 hands of horsepower and horse sense.

On chilly mornings when Blue didn't buckle down, the three old girls were not above corporal punishment. They'd nip him hard, or knock him with a shoulder whenever the need arose. They did more to train him to the disciplines of logging than Shaylee ever could. The mares made sure he pulled his weight and held steady when the chips were down.

Still and all, today Shaylee wished Blue weren't part of her backup team. Things were going very well with the grays, but it was time to give them a break and replace them with the blue roans. This particular patch of woods was hilly so the going was rough. The landing area, where the day's logs were stacked until trucked to the mill, was a long pull downhill from them. The load was unsteady as Gracie and Gabrielle picked their way down a narrow gap through the forest, one that was covered with dead fir needles. One slip or misstep and a log could start sliding downhill, thousands of pounds in an avalanche behind the horses.

Shaylee trotted beside the pulled logs, behind the team, controlling the mares with twenty-foot reins. She remained vigilant of the terrain as she clucked, geed, hawed and whoaed in constant communication, giving them as much guidance as she could. Hers was a constant dance, leaping back and forth across the logs to stay out of the bite, the space between a standing tree and the logs, a space where she could easily be crushed. But it was the team's own strength and determination that navigated them safely down the hillside.

A cohort had been damaged in a location like this. He was coming down a slope when the heavy rain began to form rivulets everywhere. He knew better than to continue, but wanted to make just that one last run. The pull started to slide, jamming into his one horse hitch, then rotating to sideswipe the teamster as well. His leg had been shattered that day.

He recovered, but the horse was a loss. Shaylee considered this a sin.

She shook her head to jiggle the memory away once she entered the clearing at the base of the hill. A logging road ended here so it was a good landing space for her operation. Shaylee directed Gracie and Gabrielle to position the logs near the others they'd already gathered.

While Shaylee unhooked and fed the team, young Jamie Farrell bucked the logs to length. Then he grappled them onto two slender poles that lay perpendicular under them. He rolled the logs across the poles to join the others in a neat, growing pile. This made an easy catch for the self-loading truck at the end of each day. It was the kind of precision that locals had come to expect from Shaylee's horse logging operation.

Each time she saw Jamie, Shaylee was tickled by the fiery redness of his hair. She imagined he'd been teased enough about it as a child to account for his shyness. He was new on her crew, not quite out of his teens, but she was impressed. He was tough and willing to learn, even if he was too clumsy for his own good.

Jack Bergstrom half-slid half-walked down the path the horses had pioneered, grabbing boughs to slow his speed. Once at the landing, he restarted his chain saw to give Jamie a hand. Jack, a crafty logger when he wasn't holding down a barstool, worked ahead of Shaylee in the woods, felling, delimbing and topping the trees they selected.

Today they felled only diseased, broken and dead trees. This was the type of work that kept horse loggers in business, in fact had them on the increase once again. A team could pinpoint certain growth without disturbing the rest. "There won't be much value from this stand. Firewood mainly," Shaylee had warned the owner of this scruffy acreage.

"I'm mostly interested in improving conditions for the healthy trees," he'd replied, adding that he also wanted to promote growth for the mushroom hunters who collected wild morels, matsutakes and chanterelles for the local markets.

Shaylee opened the lunch she'd packed for the three of them. *Left on their own, men pack Fritos and Ho-Hos.* She'd made pasties with a recipe from Welsh miners in the Upper Peninsula of Michigan where her mother had worked the white pine decades ago. Properly wrapped, the delicious crusty pies, filled with ground meat, potatoes, onions, and carbs stayed warm for half a day in a worker's lunch. Shaylee handed two to Jack and two to Jamie, then unwrapped one for herself.

"There's an extra one here if you need it," she said to the younger man.

Jamie smiled shyly. They ate in silent camaraderie, sharing a Thermos of coffee and bottles of water. They listened to the nearby creek, an irate chickadee, the breeze rustling the hemlocks and fir, the horses taking on fuel and stomping their massive hooves to shoo away flies. The breeze also chased away the odor of horse sweat.

When she finished her pasty and an apple, Shaylee stood, stretched her back and looked up the gap where the horses had dragged the logs down. She'd wander up that way and find a place to pee.

Half way up the gap Shaylee felt a chill. Maybe the breeze had come up, cooling her after a hard morning of work. But no. That wasn't it. In fact, the rustling in the trees had stopped. There was no sound of wind or birdcall either. Even her own passage seemed muted. The forest was never this silent. It was still, too still, like the hushed seconds between the lowering of house lights and actors appearing on a stage. Tense seconds of anticipation.

Shaylee's skin prickled and her downy arm hairs stood. She'd hoped what she'd been told would be no more than a prediction, a concocted prophecy, a baseless dream. But she knew now that, step by step, she was walking into a deadly reality.

One more tread, and she saw it. She froze. The skeleton must have been uncovered by the skidding logs. Bones were scattered and the skull had been crushed, but shards were there. Enough to know it was human. Shreds of clothing confirmed it.

Shaken by the sight, Shaylee had one thought as she placed a call to 911.

I knew this would happen.

* * *

That night, alone at home, Shaylee spoke to her reflection in the mirror after she'd showered. "Two nights ago, First Female told me I'd find a body, that's how I knew. I hoped it was a dream. But I was wrong."

Fortunately, her reflection looked back but didn't *talk* back. No shape shifting or anything like that. Always the same mess of freckles, unruly strawberry blonde curls, violet eyes. She looked exactly like herself, but that didn't mean she was the only one home. Anything was possible. As a youngster, she'd been abused by Uncle Carson and cousin Chad often enough to know that was the reason emotional problems dogged her into adulthood. It didn't take years of counseling to explain why she'd rather work far in the woods than in town surrounded by crowds.

Her dissociation happened mostly at night so she told herself she was just dreaming. But these dreams were so real that they had to be more than increased brain activity during REM phases. She might awaken gasping for breath as if she'd been running a marathon. Crying like a banshee.

"Shirsh Shemale ish nodda dream," Shaylee told her image while she brushed her teeth, foaming at the mouth. She'd been wide awake when First Female made herself known two nights ago, after so many years of silence.

Shaylee spit and added, "At least I think I was."

She'd been a frightened twelve-year-old hiding from her cousin behind hay bales in the loft when she first heard from the Presence. The calming voice came as whispery music in Shaylee's ears from all directions at once, breathy and sweet as a woodwind at the lowest end of its range. It shushed her and told her the boy would cause her no more pain.

Later, the body of cousin Chad had been found where he'd fallen from the loft into the stable below.

The stallion in the stall had been terrified when the bully's body plummeted from above. If the fall hadn't killed Chad, sharp hooves crushing his spine had done the trick.

The law questioned little Shaylee Ward back then, wondering whether she had the strength to push the husky farm boy out of the loft. Her mother finally gathered up enough sense to move her a long way away from Uncle Carson and the rest of the family. Shaylee had begun to mend, and in time, she'd nearly forgotten the voice of First Female.

Nearly forgotten. Then, two nights ago, Shaylee had been sitting alone cross-legged on her bed, surrounded by bills too numerous to count on all her digits. She'd exploded, "How can new horse blankets possibly cost more than my quarterly taxes?"

Someone answered. "Consider the value the best blanket has to the horse."

Shaylee whipped her head around so fast she nearly cracked her neck. Bills scattered. Whether the speaker was in the room or in her head, she was invisible. Fear trickled down Shaylee's spine.

When the Presence spoke again, Shaylee recognized First Female's voice from that terrible time in the barn when she was twelve. It had soothed her then in the way of music. Now, First Female spoke of a spirit coming to rectify certain wrongs. An image of a girl on the back of an enormous flying bear appeared before Shaylee's eyes ... or was it behind them?

"Her name is Cascadia. You will teach her things about humans that Old Man Above and I do not understand. She will be sent to you soon. When she is ready. When you are ready."

Are you fucking kidding me? Why me? I barely have myself under control much less someone even more confused about human behavior than I am.

The Presence explained it was time for Shaylee to pay back a debt. She was to help First Female, just as she had been helped as a child. Help even if it put her in danger. "Your first mission will be to help Cascadia discover why human girls are being murdered in our forest. You will soon find the body of such a one."

That was exactly what had happened. Shaylee recalled this conversation while she, Jack and Jamie had waited for law enforcement to investigate the skeleton at the logging site. She'd said nothing about it to anyone. Who'd believe it? But she knew other girls would be found, too.

Something evil was loose in her woods. Police methods alone weren't the answer. Bones and teeth were too scattered, too little physical evidence was left after weasels and insects had eaten their fill. A murderer would go free unless something superhuman intervened. First Female had chosen her to help. She had a debt to pay. And so Shaylee committed.

When Cascadia is ready I'll be waiting.

CHAPTER THREE

"Who is he?" Cascadia asked, looking at the man out cold at Helen of Troy's gold sandaled feet.

"His name is Jim Bowie."

"Why is he here?"

"First Female selected him from the Tree of Human History. He is here to teach you the skill of the knife. No other human was ever his match at hitting a target with a thrown blade. But your smelly bear has frightened his horse half to death."

The buckskin had reared when it saw Silver Tip and thrown the man roughly to the ground. Helen shook her head, then tucked up an ebony tendril that had come loose from the golden hairnet. "I've met Jim before. He's not all that easygoing even on a good day. Now he'll really be peevish. Go find his horse."

But Cascadia stood rooted to the meadow floor, staring at the unconscious man. She'd never been able to study a human male at such close range before. He was a six-footer, not heavy but stocky as if he were one bundle of bulked-up muscle. His long sideburns and thick wavy hair were deep chestnut, but his skin, although roughened from exposure to sun and wind, was fair. The cleft in his chin and his square jaw aroused a feeling in Cascadia similar to the one she felt with Dogoda, the West Wind.

29

"That horse will be easier to catch if you start while it's still in the same hemisphere," Helen snapped. She knelt beside Jim Bowie's unconscious body, placing her hand on his forehead.

"Yes, yes. I'm going," Cascadia said. "But why is he dressed so strangely?" His clothes looked different from any she had seen. The human men she'd observed mostly wore jeans and drab weatherproof jackets or camouflage fatigues. This stranger's woolen coat was waist length in the front and knee length in the back. There was no language written on his shirt. It was snow white, held in place by a black bow at the collar and tucked under a waist length vest. On his belt at his right hip he wore a sheath with the largest knife Cascadia had ever seen.

She breathed deeply. "His odor is strange. I like it."

"Yes. Clove and citrus. Jim's quite the dandy. Likes a tonsorial parlor. I'd say they've been liberal with the cologne," Helen explained. "He came here from the 1800s. The Texas territories. It's how well-to-do men dressed then, long before the Alamo."

"The Alamo?"

Helen looked up and waved her hands in a gesture to be gone. "More talk later. Now go find that flighty beast."

Cascadia took one more glance before rushing to locate the horse. The way Bowie looked, the way he smelled. She liked both. But her greatest interest in him was the skill he would teach. She'd never held a knife much less thrown one. The idea was exciting.

30

By the time she returned with the buckskin in tow, Bowie was sitting up, leaning against the base of a massive red cedar, staring bleary eyed at the goddess. Helen was holding a ladle to his lips. The bubbly pink liquid in it smelled so much worse than skunk or dung, it nearly overpowered Cascadia. Silver Tip pawed at his nose and disappeared into the woods. His departure pleased the horse who turned her rump to the two-leggers and began to graze.

"Nectar of the Gods," Helen said to Cascadia, indicating the mucus-like liquid in the ladle. "It will bring him back if only because it tastes as wretched as it smells. If I had enough of it, I could make him immortal. But then the Alamo would never happen. And Texas would be Mexico. And Old Man Above would throw a hissy fit about goddesses who alter the least little bit of history without his say so."

"What is that you speak?" Bowie asked in a voice spiked with pain. "To whom do you speak it?" He was still too weak and woozy to look around and see the spirit standing still as a statue at the edge of the meadow.

"Is this refreshment some manner of piss?" His speech was as strange to Cascadia as his clothes.

Bowie rubbed his eyes with his fists and made an effort to stand. He wobbled but succeeded. Once stable, he gathered up his flat-crowned hat and dusted off the wide felt brim. Finally, he said to Helen, "Lovely as always, my dear." He targeted a kiss in her direction but either she turned her head slightly or his aim was still faulty from his fall.

"There is another here. And she is very interested in you." She gave Cascadia a small smile, grabbed Bowie's square jaw and pointed his head toward the spirit.

Cascadia had forgotten that when this human male looked at her he would see his idea of the most spectacular woman in the world. And because of her interest in him, she would see herself as he saw her. All the colors she had inhaled from Helen's elixir seemed to vibrate within her. Warm, exhilarating.

Ouch! Something nipped at her waist. As she sucked in her breath, her ribs felt like they were being crushed. She looked down at her body and saw that she was trussed in a revealing contraption of lace and bone.

Helen saw it, too. "Ah, Jim, you sly dog. A corset? And such a pretty one!"

"God's teeth and toenails," Jim Bowie gasped, openly gawking at his fantasy in the flesh. "I must still be in the arms of Morpheus, or I am dead and gone to heaven."

Cascadia watched his cool gray eyes open wider, his back straighten, and a beguiling smile lift his craggy face. He moved a hand to cover the front of his trousers with his hat, there where the heavy wool seemed to be rising on its own accord. "No, indeed. Not dead."

Bowie's infectious grin evoked a response from the spirit. She did not smile back, but her breasts reacted in a way that could hardly be considered spiritual. A drawstring strained across her chest where the lacy edge of a chemise peeked over the corset. The get-up pushed her breasts high and round. They were totally uncovered on the upper half, except where golden ringlets from her head cascaded over her nakedness. The chemise was longer than her corset and covered the very top of her thighs.

Cascadia could not see her own face, of course, but based on this human's hungry expression and Helen's mischievous one, she must be a looker.

"Mr. Bowie," Helen said. "May I present Cascadia, your student for the Skill of the Knife. Cassie, my dear, Mr. Bowie is one of the Skill Masters who will teach you physical combat techniques just as we goddesses teach emotional ones. You will need both to succeed in your endeavors among the humans."

"How ... how do you do, Miss Cassie," Bowie said with a bow. "The pleasure is all mine, encountering such a dandizette here in the wilderness."

In a gesture Cascadia could not control, she curtsied low. She thought her breasts might pop free and bobble in the breeze. "Monsieur," she uttered.

Monsieur?

As Cascadia rose from her curtsy, Helen handed her a whisper of fabric. "Put these on. Panties weren't worn in the early 1800s so I've just invented you a pair."

Helen turned to the man as Cascadia shimmied into the French cuts. The goddess said sternly, "Now see here, Mr. Bowie. There are important tasks to be done. Put your mind on business, please. Or must I advise Old Man Above of your licentious conduct?"

"No, my dear. He's well aware of it. But begin we must and in haste. I need soon return to Texas where all is not well. Thunder builds to the south." He glanced once again at the spirit. "But, Miss Cassie, you sorely test a man's resolve."

* * *

In the next few invigorating days, Cascadia's Skill Master was relentless, and she thrived on every moment of it. She'd done nothing but observe for so long that mastering a difficult skill made her giddy with pleasure.

Bowie's lessons began with a lecture. He told her a knife was more useful than a gun. "A knife is always loaded," he said, giving her a flash of that crooked smile before becoming resolute in his instructions. He explained the knife's place in history as man's first manufactured weapon, and he told her stories of great warriors armed with nothing but shields and blades to defend their homelands. She'd had no idea humans could be so … so magnificent.

Maybe there is hope for this species yet.

Jim taught her the strengths and weaknesses of different blades and handles, from daggers to switchblades. He was well acquainted with weaponry used before and even after his lifespan on earth, providing her with the most recent and treacherous of technology.

One evening early in her training, Cascadia was bathing in her pool and telling Silver Tip how he'd have to learn to lower his head when she threw blades from his back. Helen of Troy appeared on her favorite boulder.

34

"Jim Bowie says you are a good student. A quick learner."

"Skill Master Bowie is a good teacher," the spirit replied. He seemed stern to her and never commented on her progress, so she was tickled with Helen's comment.

"He said he's never met a woman so willing to learn without employing backtalk. I told him that's because you're not a real woman. He laughed at me and said if I think you're not a real woman, I must never have looked at you." She pushed out her lower lip. "I must say, if I weren't your mentor, I would be jealous. He used to covet me that way."

"If the Skill Master covets me, you have done your job well," Cascadia answered.

Helen laughed. "Your tongue is as pleasing as your aspect, little one."

The spirit was glad she pleased Helen as well as Bowie. Knowing he'd complimented her knife skill gratified her far more than his interest in her body. "He has not said such things to me."

"He's captivated by you and is probably fighting the attraction. Lust between teacher and student is usually frowned upon. But in this case, First Female considers it instructive."

"If he doesn't want to have lust with me, why would it be hard for him to avoid it?"

Helen threw back her lovely head and laughed again. Then she said, "You really are an unbaked biscotti aren't you? I think it's time for your next lesson in the Skill of Lust. And I think I'll allow Mr. Bowie to be my guest lecturer for that."

The next day, Jim had his hand on Cascadia's, closed over a knife handle. "It's the basic grip. Thumb on top, like you're holding a hammer." He stood behind her as he spoke. She felt warmth in her hair and realized it was his breath. The smell of spice from his cologne made her lean back into him.

His hand slid from hers up to her wrist where he grasped her firmly. "Tense your wrist and bend your elbow to a ninety degree angle." He led her through the motion until the knife pointed forward with the sharp side of the blade downward. "From this position you can decide to jab or throw. Today, you will throw at the knot in that tree."

He raised her tense arm, bending it backwards until the upper part was parallel to her head. She peeked back and into his eyes.

"Look ahead," he barked. "Concentrate. Now snap your arm forward and release." The knife flew but missed the target tree altogether.

She felt the heat of a blush in her cheeks and said, "I can do better."

"You must," he answered as he retrieved the weapon. "Human lives will depend on it." They tried it again. And again until she had the grip and throw under control.

At the end of the session, Bowie did not move away. Cascadia started to turn, but he stopped her, wrapped his arms around her. This time – this close – his breath tickled her ear. Tiny bumps appeared on her naked arms.

How strange.

He pulled her tight against his chest with his left arm around her waist, fingers downward on her stomach pushing her backside against him. She felt him harden against her buttocks. With his right hand he reached from behind her and untied the taut drawstring on the chemise. Then he pushed his fingers under the snowy cotton to run them along the top of the corset where it lifted her breasts. His fingers grazed one nipple then pushed around to cup the other breast in his hand with his arm still pressing against the first.

Cascadia's nipples became as hard as two shiny brown acorns. "They're hard," she exclaimed. "How funny this body is!"

"This body is anything but funny," he answered and it seemed to her that his voice was lower, huskier than it had been. His breathing was heavier, and so was hers.

Are we becoming ill? It's as though we were running.

Jim moved back enough to unlace her corset, and it dropped to the ground. She sighed. It was such a pleasure to have all restraint gone. The loose chemise felt so free. Jim spun her toward him, and she dropped the knife to the ground. He pulled her against him, and she could feel his hardness bulging under the wool trousers.

"Is this your lust?" she asked, giving it a slight squeeze.

"So it is," gasped Bowie. She watched as he unhooked his vest and the suspenders underneath. His trousers dropped but the long shirt hid his erection from her sight.

"I want to see." She began to push the material aside, but his need was so urgent, she had no time to see more. He swept her up and crushed his lips to hers. She wrapped her legs around his strong body. With help from an obliging tree for support, he pushed between her legs. She thought it would hurt, that he had it all wrong since none of the animals she'd observed did this face to face. It did make her cry out at first, but then the stretch and slide felt good. Very good. As sweet as the honey made by the meadow bees.

He moved deeper, and she pushed toward him. She was enthralled, and very glad that Helen of Troy had invented undies that were crotchless.

In upcoming days, the spirit learned to throw, thrust, attack and defend, both with a knife and with sex. Bowie taught her, "Disable the eyes, and you stop the man in his tracks." He gave her anatomy lessons in the most vulnerable kill points. She learned to hit them with absolute accuracy every time.

After practicing with the knife, Cascadia and Jim Bowie practiced their more intimate thrusting skills. "What are you teaching me now?" she would ask as he kissed her in surprising places and held her in unexpected ways. Sometimes it was rough or then again as gentle as rocking in a cradle. The spirit discovered that humans were far more imaginative in the lust department than the other animals she'd watched.

I will have much to show Dogoda, the West Wind, next autumn when he returns.

When they would lie together, sweaty and exhausted between dances, Bowie would sometimes tell her about his life. How he'd amassed a fortune as a land speculator and slave trader, long before he'd become known for prowess with a knife. "My brother Rezin had the knife forged for me."

"Have you killed with it?"

"Some say I killed bears. But never a bear the size of yours."

"I mean humans."

"I've killed a man who needed killing, to be sure. And I'll likely kill more."

He'd had many women, from back alley dance halls to ladies' parlors. He'd even become a Mexican citizen so he could marry the governor's daughter. But he told the spirit he'd never had any woman like her, so willing to deliver more than was asked. "In my experience in the 1800s, women are far more reserved than you."

"Human women must be bound by customs I haven't learned from Helen. Or from you. Neither of you is a teacher of inhibition."

Jim chuckled. "No, Helen and I have not given you the usual traditions. I've taught you how to kill a man. She taught you how to lure him close enough to do it. Judging by your mastery of our lessons, you are a prodigy in the skill department. You have the power to do great things if the gods so choose."

Sometimes she would watch as Jim slept, his thick hair tousled forward and his eyelids trembling with a dream. She knew the Skill Master had been captured by her, his student. She was aware that his feeling for her had moved from lust to something he called love. He had first said it when she was teasing him with her tongue, an intimacy that Helen taught her. Then he'd taken to whispering his love as he held her in the night, telling her he did not want to return to his own wife in his own time. He wished to stay with her forever.

She wondered how such love must feel. Was it what she sensed for Dogoda? Maybe it was how she felt about the land that was her namesake and her drive to protect it. But for now, her arousal by a human male ended with orgasm, nothing more. He had fallen hard but she not at all.

When the last days came, it was painful for Bowie. He simply did not want to give her up. Once Cascadia knew all she needed about knife combat, however, First Female severed the relationship with a cutting edge all her own. She ordered Helen of Troy to tell Bowie that his wife and children were dying of cholera. He was needed at home immediately.

"Know this," Helen told him. "You will not grieve for the love you have found here with Cascadia. When you are back home in your own time, you will have no memory of her. Instead, you will mourn the loss of your own family. But it will end soon. You will die a hero and be revered by your nation forever. It's as close to immortality as a human can get."

Cascadia and Silver Tip watched from the trees as Jim Bowie mounted his buckskin and galloped away, back into time. She'd learned a great deal about knives, but she had none of her own. At least until she returned to her pool. On a boulder beside it she found a beautiful white leather sheath on a belt. In the sheath was a slender and elegant killing weapon. It was the perfect weight, balance and size for her hand. The knife was a double edged dagger with a golden guard and bone handle.

"It is a gift designed just for you by Jim Bowie, although I have added a property of my own," said First Female in her surround-sound voice. Then she told Cascadia the magic property imbued in the knife.

That night, the spirit no longer had Bowie for warmth, so she leaned against Silver Tip. She'd learned about more than knives. She'd learned that she could use human desire as a weapon, a tool even older than knives. She'd completed her first course in the skills of lust and the knife. It was time for her mission to begin.

CHAPTER FOUR

Shaylee Ward's logging team took the weekend off. The rain and fog sucked, but more than that, the mares - Gabrielle, Ghost and Violet - needed a good rest, proper grooming and as much hay as they could burn. Jamie would see that they got it. The teenager had a special affection for the horses, and they for him. Meanwhile, Jack would visit his favorite barstools at taverns around town.

Blue, the youngest Percheron, needed exercise. Shaylee knew he was not yet a team player but excelled at working on his own. He was perfect for her secret job. It was an obligation few people knew about. Even Jamie had no real notion where the two went, only that they would return in a couple days. Shaylee knew he was curious, and she liked the kid all the more for not asking questions.

"It's for a good cause," was all she told him.

"Glad to hear it," was all he answered.

Saturday morning at dawn, he helped Shaylee load a two hundred pound generator into a cart. The genny fit snugly against a large cedar box filled with foodstuffs. Shaylee had customized the cart by cutting down a standard utility trailer and adding fat tires that could climb up rugged hills or over windfalls. She'd fashioned a hitch for Blue's harness at one end of the cart and a sturdy platform at the other where she could stand. She'd gotten the idea from dog sleds. If the pull became difficult for the muscular young horse, she could step down and walk beside or behind the cart.

Jamie and Shaylee rolled the loaded cart up a ramp and into the horse trailer in a second stall alongside Blue. She jumped into the cab of her pick-up, calling "See you Monday."

"Be careful," Jamie yelled over his shoulder as he returned to the barn.

Shaylee drove into the forest on a road as rough as a washboard from tire chains on heavy trucks. Eventually, she turned onto an abandoned logging track narrow enough for her horse trailer to be swept by tree boughs on both sides. She parked where even that trail turned to bush. Only elk and deer traffic maintained it from here.

Shaylee unloaded the gelding, avoiding his smart aleck nips as she harnessed him in seventy pounds of leather and metal. After linking his harness to the rig, she used him to unload the cart from the trailer. Giving the load a final check for even weight distribution, she clucked to Blue. He eagerly began to pull down the deer path into the forest.

The drizzle was largely held off by the fir and cedar canopy, but it was a damp, unwelcoming morning. Shaylee turned her collar up and her hat brim down as she trotted along to keep pace with Blue. He was feeling fresh and sassy.

"You'll slow down soon enough, youngster," she said to him. She jumped up on the back platform and performed a balancing act as the cart snaked around thickets or over fallen logs. Blue knew enough to measure the room he had between trees and to choose the best footing for himself without upsetting the load. Shaking his head and blowing, he clearly preferred this to the boring job of following another team.

In time, the rain splattered more urgently on the leaves and fir needles all around her. A chill settled in as though ice water trickled down her spine. Shaylee whoaed Blue then dug an oversized slicker and knee high rain boots out of the cart. Once she was encased in the heavy gear, she stopped all motion to listen. She'd never met anyone in this part of the woods, but she stayed on the alert. When sure they were alone, she clucked Blue onward. "We don't want anyone following us to them, do we?" She watched his ears turn toward her. "They've had enough trouble."

Shaylee was well aware the forests of Cascadia were home to more than one kind of human. There were groups of survivalists, homeless camps of vulnerable families, drug runners, bands of pickers illegally harvesting the forest's bounty, and even damaged war vets more at home in the wild than in society. Most were benign, wanting only solitude. Others were predators.

Shaylee was taking the generator and supplies to a band of women who had formed their own compound at an abandoned farm carved from a meadow. Each was in hiding for a reason of her own. Many were battered wives or stalked prey or abuse victims on the run. They maintained their own land, raised their own crops, guarded their own borders and bothered no one. Shaylee helped by bringing in supplies. This monthly mission through the woods was important to her, even though the trail required a long pull up a steep grade. "Maybe we should be rock climbers," she said, jumping from one slippery boulder to another.

They'd traveled several miles when the rain began to hammer them harder. Shaylee judged it to be over half way to her destination so it made more sense to continue than go back. Blue's massive haunches dug in and carried them onward over decomposing hemlock logs and through dense thickets of vine maples. As his body warmed to the task, the odor of sweaty wet horse assaulted Shaylee's nose.

At last they arrived at a creek where a gurgle of water flowed over a gravelly bottom. In dry seasons, it had no water at all. It cut nicely between rock outcroppings, making a smooth incline for the big horse, circumventing a difficult climb through some of the densest forest. Walking right up the creek bed was their usual route.

Shaylee negotiated Blue into the creek where he stopped for a drink. The water swept across his hooves today. As soon as he was ready they moved on, the cart bouncing along the gravel bed. Shaylee stood on the back platform out of the water.

After an hour, though, real alarm clutched at her stomach, replacing the mere butterflies that had been fluttering there. The flow of water was becoming a current. It splashed nearly to Blue's knees and threatened the sides of the wagon. But the creek banks were now too high for them to climb out.

"What do you think, Blue? Should we turn around?" Shaylee called loudly over the roar of water rushing through a narrow channel. Even as she said it she knew there wasn't enough room to do it. Besides, the women really needed the generator and the food. And she had to get this errand done now to be back at work by Monday.

Blue arched his neck, tucked in his head and splashed onward, concentrating on the job. He was a better worker on his own terms than in a team. "Guess you could say the same for me, my friend," Shaylee yelled.

To lessen the weight on Blue, she stepped off the back platform into the current. The force of it nearly toppled her, but she struggled forward to be sure the provisions were still covered by the tarps, dry and safe. She splashed on ahead until she was beside Blue. He shook water from his neck like a massive dog and nickered at her, muscling his way upstream as Shaylee thrashed along beside him, grabbing limbs and snags in the water to pull herself forward. It was exhausting. Strong as she was from years as a logger she couldn't keep it up for long.

"What do you think? Do we need to leave the wagon here? Go on without it?" She peered through the blinding downpour for a place to moor the wagon so they could come back for it when the water level went down.

Nothing.

None of the snags sticking out of the creek was strong enough to hold. The wagon would break loose and founder. The banks were a steep rise of earth held together by webs of sedge, dagger leaf and other wild grasses. The top of the muddy banks ended at the base of the volcanic rock walls. Shaylee could climb it, but Blue would never get up that bank with or without the wagon. And she would never leave him.

"Just a little further, Blue. Up ahead it's low enough for us to climb out. Promise." She shivered from cold. And fear.

Without warning, the cart jerked to a halt, throwing Blue off balance. He nearly fell, caught himself, then reared back. The enormous animal tried to pitch forward again. But he couldn't move. A ton of horse was on the verge of panic.

Shaylee ducked to avoid flailing hooves the size of platters. "Steady, Blue. It's just caught on a snag. Whoa now. I can fix this." She moved in closer to stroke his neck. Her voice calmed him. "It's okay. I'll go look."

When she turned to go back to the cart, the current pushed her from behind. She stumbled on an unseen rock and fell to her knees. Grabbing for the wagon, Shaylee struggled back up but her boots filled with water. She kicked out of them. The cold was such a shock to her feet that she nearly didn't feel the gravel cutting into them.

She was reaching for the obstruction under the wagon when a voice yelled, "You must get to higher ground now. A flash flood is coming."

Holy shit!

She whirled around. Through the rain, she saw no one. She shielded her eyes and squinted to the top of the bank. In a flash of lightning she clearly saw the terrifying mass of an immense grizzly leaping from the bank into the swell below.

The bear hit the water at her side.

I'm dead.

Her only defense was the ball bat she kept in the cart, far out of reach. Terror paralyzed her. The bear was so massive he blocked everything else from her view. She shrieked as his hot, fetid breath strafed her face.

"Get into the wagon."

Shaylee then saw a human form through the deluge, a rider on the monster's back. She fought through her fear to remember the vision that First Female had projected before her eyes: a spirit on a flying bear. She instantly obeyed, scrambling onto the cedar food box.

The bear thrust deep into the water with an enormous forearm, coming up with a paw full of tangled roots. He did it again. Suddenly the cart lurched forward as Blue was free to pull away.

The horse, sensing the bear, tried now to run. Every instinct he had said this predator meant death. If he panicked he would upset the wagon, lose the load and maybe even drown.

"Horse, be calm. Silver Tip will not hurt you," ordered the rider whose soft voice could somehow be heard over the roaring water. And like magic, the horse responded. Blue settled, arched his neck once again and calmly began to pull. The bear put a shoulder against the back of the cart and pushed it forward, helping the horse avoid more snags. The

only one still buzzing with fear was Sh█
on tight, as if the wagon were a life raft.

"He will not hurt you either, my familiar."

Yeah, sure. Scared of a bear? Not me.

Working together the animals reached a bend where the creek widened, the bank lowered, and the water was less deadly. The drenched party climbed out. All four stood gasping and staring at each other.

Shaylee felt as waterlogged and exhausted as a Titanic refugee. The adrenaline that had pumped through her system now drained and her knees wobbled. Her rescue team looked nearly as disheveled, a smallish plain woman-like spirit and an ancient bear whose years could be counted by the gray in his fur. A bear apparently as vicious as a duckling.

So this duo is my destiny.

Finally, Shaylee said, "I'm glad you think paws-itive."

"I what?" Cascadia asked. "You are my human familiar, but I already do not understand."

"Paws-itive. *Think PAWS-itive.* Like your t-shirt says under the drawing of the bear track."

"My t-shirt spoke to you?"

"No, no, no. That's what's written on it."

"Oh! I wondered what the hieroglyphics said. Thank you."

"Any time." Shaylee breathed deep, helping the last of her fear dissipate. "From here we can climb a trail up the cliff away from the creek. There's a stand of black willows halfway up. Let's get there. They'll be above the flood line and keep us dry."

…ee. She held

HISTORY OF CASCADIA

to shelter the human, the
…ar from the storm. Shaylee
…e quickness of a person at
… shed her slicker then noticed
…hirt that was dry. This one was
across her chest. Shaylee didn't
… the crude joke but did wonder if
First r… …t give her this dry-clothes-magic-
thingy, too.

They sat on the tarp Shaylee spread on the ground. She checked her feet for damage from the creek bed, finding only a couple of cuts and scrapes. For a long time, the spirit and the human listened to the rain and stared at Blue and Silver Tip. The two animals stood nose to nose.

"The horse accepts him," the spirit finally observed. "I know another that was terrified by him."

If you weren't here, I'd be terrified of him, too.

"I've never seen anything like it. Maybe Blue's just glad to have another guy around since he works with mares all day." She was crunching a power bar and an apple, wishing the snack was a burger and fries. The spirit had refused food.

Maybe she lives on air.

"Maybe the bear tells him important things," Cascadia said.

"Whatever, it's a pretty odd couple." The young horse and old bear did seem to be enjoying some juicy bit of gossip.

"You think they are a couple? They will lust together?"

Shaylee choked back a laugh which escaped as a sort of a snort. "Lust? No, not that kind of couple. They just like each other."

"You humans are confusing."

Look who's talking.

Shaylee snuck another glance at the spirit. She'd seen faces on mannequins that were more animated. There were no lines, no scars, no freckles. Nothing that makes individual faces unique. It was just so, so average. She crossed her legs, leaned forward and asked, "Now that you've saved my horse and my ass, why are you here?"

"Helen sent me to ask your help in finding a man. It is my first mission as arranged by First Female."

"Helen?"

"Helen of Troy."

"Helen of Troy! Sure she did." Shaylee was used to dissociation. It was a gift from her own traumatic past. Certainly, she was no stranger to peculiar thoughts and visions. She'd never gone so far as to develop multiple personalities, but she could 'awaken' in an unexpected place or even lose time. Her dreams were often sharper than her reality. But this? This was too weird.

Maybe this whole damn thing isn't really happening.

Cascadia said, "Helen worried you might not believe. But First Female told her you are open to the unknown."

"Well, you certainly qualify."

"She said that you would explain to me the things we spirits don't understand."

Shaylee sighed. "So tell me what you want from me."

"You discovered bones. Human bones."

Shaylee remembered the pathetic skeleton her horse team had uncovered in the woods. The one First Female had said she would find. "Sometimes hikers get lost in the forest and die of exposure. Animals eat the remains."

"The woman that lived in that body was not a hiker. She picked mushrooms. She picked salal." Cascadia had observed these things.

Shaylee nodded. "There are crews brought to the forest to harvest crops. It's mostly illegal. Maybe half the salal used in rose bouquets comes from public lands."

"These pickers are criminals?"

Shaylee shrugged. "Well, they're hard working and poor, brought here to do the labor. The real criminals are the crew bosses who bring them. They stay away from my logging outfit, but I've seen them sometimes herding their pickers from one place to another."

"Do you know a man with a scraggly grey beard and a machete that he uses to cut underbrush?"

Shaylee smiled briefly. "That describes maybe half the men in the Pacific Northwest."

"His belly is large and he has a tarantula crawling toward his ear."

A bad taste exploded in Shaylee's mouth. "Ah, yes. That's Spider. I don't know his real name, but I've seen him in bars around River Junction. The tarantula on his neck is a tat."

"Tat?"

"A tattoo. Some humans have artwork inked on their bodies."

"Ah. So tattoo men are bad humans. That is easy for me to understand."

"No, most of them aren't bad. They just like tats."

If a plain Jane can look crestfallen, the spirit did. "Then a tat is no hint of badness. But this man hurts women, has lust with them, then kills them."

Shaylee's jaw tightened. Were the bones she'd found the work of Spider? This was the kind of scumbag she wanted to keep away from the women's compound. "Sounds like he's attacking members of a picking crew. He could even be the crew boss."

"Why does a crew not stop him from attacking their women?" Cascadia asked.

Cascadia looked guileless. Shaylee tried to accept that the spirit really didn't know, and that First Female intended Shaylee to explain it.

How can I do that when I understand so little about men myself?

She had to try. "The pickers need him to provide the work. It's all they have to feed their families. So they can't turn on him. And they can't go to the authorities since they shouldn't be in these woods themselves."

"And that is why nobody avenges these women." A cloud crossed the spirit's face. Shaylee wondered if it was fear or anger. Or maybe it was Cascadia's first understanding of something ugly. "Nobody knows who the women are. They are poor and weak with nobody watching out for them." Shaylee stopped short of telling Cascadia that authorities might not care even if they knew.

"So men have lust for them?"

"Well, there is more than one kind of lust. Some is about sex, but some is about power or domination. Sometimes it all gets mixed up."

"But why would a human choose to destroy one of your own kind?"

There's the conundrum of the ages!

"That's a question with so many answers that nobody has them all. All I know is what I know. Some people are sick, some are damaged. Different backgrounds lead to different behaviors. There are people who put their own needs over the needs of all others. Most would deny being evil. But given the right set of circumstances, it is wise for all women and children to be leery of all men until their truth is known."

Cascadia nodded and stood. "This is what you call sad, I think."

Shaylee followed suit. "Guess First Female intends us to discover answers together."

"Together. And now we must confront this man. Where will we find him?'

Shaylee's muscles clenched. "Did you say *we*?"

"Yes and soon."

"Okay. But I need to deliver these supplies to living women before I investigate dead ones."

"A reasonable request. Silver Tip and I will wait until you are ready."

"Well it isn't really a request. It's what I'm going ..." Shaylee stopped. She realized Blue and she were alone once more.

CHAPTER FIVE

The first workers imported to pick forest crops in parts of Cascadia were Asians. Some died from eating poisonous mushrooms that looked like an edible fungus from their homeland. The workers were mostly Latinos now. Shaylee wondered if that was why River Junction had more than its fair share of both Chinese and Mexican restaurants.

She thought about it while plunging downhill through the woods, brushing boughs out of the way. She'd delivered the generator to the women's compound the night before and was on her way home when Silver Tip appeared again beside the trail. Blue and the bear had another good chin wag, the horse nickering in delight and the bear answering with an 'ar, ar ar.'

It made Shaylee laugh, this strange kinship. Then Cascadia giggled, too, right next to her ear.

"Holy crap!" Shaylee yelped. She'd heard the voice but not seen a person until Cascadia materialized.

"I am sorry, Shaylee. I did not mean to frighten you. But I want you to know I can be invisible."

"Do you sneak up like that a lot?" Shaylee's blood pressure dropped from astronomical to even keel, and she walked on down the trail.

Apparently the spirit came with her. "First Female gave invisibility to me, but it takes energy, like creating hot or cold. You don't see it but it is there. It's tiring to generate the energy to go unseen. So I don't use it when it isn't necessary."

"Well, I prefer to see you when you approach. So nix the see-thru suit around me. Okay?"

Instantly, Cascadia was totally visible. Her *I Ain't Afraid of No Ghost* t-shirt struck Shaylee as damn appropriate for a spirit. It brought back her good humor. "Much better. Is there anything else I should know about you before you scare the shit out of me again?"

"Well, yes, maybe." Cascadia explained her skill with a knife. "Jim Bowie taught me how."

"Sure he did. With the help of Helen of Troy, I suppose."

Shaylee's sarcasm was lost on the spirit who answered, "No, not really. But Helen did teach me how to be the dream girl of any man." Cascadia explained the abilities that Helen's elixir had given her. "I don't have to be his fantasy unless I want to, though."

"Yeah? Well, I'd like to try it sometime." Shaylee had never been anyone's dream girl although she hoped her current relationship might become something of the sort. But this wasn't the time to think about Blake. Instead, she needed to think about Spider. What Cascadia had just told her helped her formulate an action plan.

That's why, two nights later, they were sitting in her pickup in the shadowy parking lot behind a local bar called Cappy's Cantina.

Shaylee was thoroughly chilled. She wished she could run the pickup's engine with the heater on thermal blast, but that would defeat their effort to keep a low profile. She glanced sideways at Cascadia, who didn't seem bothered by the temperature at all. Tonight, her shorts were dull gray and her t-shirt announced *Do I Look Like I Care?* Someday, Shaylee should teach her to read. No, maybe this was more fun.

For now, the spirit was as still as death. She was all concentration, eyes riveted on the battered back door of the cantina, waiting for her chance to act.

Shaylee had enlisted her logger Jack Bergstrom to go bar-to-bar looking for Spider. She couldn't do it herself because she didn't want the piece of crap to know she was searching for him. Besides, all it took to sign Jack up was the promise of a free glass of rot gut at every saloon they hit. Now she waited for his lanky form, a gift from his Swedish ancestors, to ramble out of Cappy's.

"Shouldn't be much longer," she muttered to Cascadia. "So far, about twenty minutes at each saloon." Shaylee had never seen Jack totally wasted. When he had a snoot full, his mustache drooped a little more and his cheeks collapsed further into his face, but he always remained upright. Like a Weeble, he wobbled but didn't fall down.

She'd introduced Jack to Cascadia earlier in the day. He'd stared at the spirit then said, "Drink like me and I guess a Swedish barmaid ain't the strangest thing you'll see."

Now Shaylee asked Cascadia, "What did he mean when he called you a Swedish barmaid?"

"His fantasy is like a Valkyrie I saw near the Chamber of Mythologies. A large yellow-haired Presence with metal horns and breasts. Although Jack's dream girl is wielding many beer steins instead of a sword."

Shaylee laughed. "How can you deal with that?"

"Since I choose to ignore it, I can see it if I wish but don't become it. The colors within me do not glow or warm. I stay who I am regardless of what men see."

And what I can see is a plain Jane.

At last the cantina's back door opened, and Jack appeared, weaving toward Shaylee's truck. She lowered her window then pulled back from the boozy surge of his breath.

"Your mark's inside. Drinking pretty heavy," Jack said, following up with a belch.

Shaylee wondered how liquored up Spider must be to qualify as a heavy drinker from Jack's point of view. "Okay, Jack. Get in. Now that you've found him, I'll take you home."

"No, ma'am. Think I'll go back inside. Keep an eye on you two." His gaze moved over to Cascadia. "Miss," he said with a tip of his hat brim before he swayed back to the cantina door.

"You remember the drill, right?" Shaylee said to Cascadia as she opened the door and slid out of the truck. "Give me ten minutes before you follow me in. Do you have a watch?"

"I will know the proper time," the spirit answered.

"All right then. Here we go."

Shaylee strutted through the front door of the cantina, head held high. She knew the importance of looking cocky even when your knees were knocking. It was the only way a woman could work so well in a field dominated by macho, macho men. The ancient fir plank that served as a bar was charred and stained from generations of cigarette butts and liquor spills. Selecting an empty stool next to the only other vacancy, Shaylee grabbed a cocktail napkin to wipe down the space in front of her, and she wrinkled her nose at the musk of sweat, sawdust, and grease that perfumed the air.

Every male eye in the place watched her, but no one made a move. Many had tried it before. Shaylee rejected each advance, or at least that was her reputation. That empty seat next to her was a no man's land. Nevertheless, a Dos Equis appeared in front of her.

"Compliments of the house," the bartender said.

"Thanks, Cappy." She knew the wee Irishman, but not why his establishment was called a cantina. Maybe it was his contribution to international détente. "Can I have a glass, too?"

"I suppose a fine lady such as yourself wants a clean one."

Shaylee laughed. She took a look around and spotted Jack, apparently dozing in a corner booth. But he nodded at her. She was glad he was there.

The cantina was half full of men whose only commonalities were sweatshirts and blood shot eyes. The tables were circular slabs cut from enormous logs and balanced on old barrels. At one of them, Spider was telling a story to three buddies. Shaylee saw the spider tat just below his left ear. Eight-leggers made her shiver but not nearly as much as this two-legger. His hands accompanied his tale in gestures as theatrical as an orchestra conductor. When he paused for a laugh from his buds, Shaylee saw him glance at her and smile. His eyes stayed cold as ball bearings.

She acknowledged the greeting with the smallest of nods. Spider was no stranger because all the people who ran crews in the woods knew each other. Besides, he'd made a failed attempt or two with her himself. He wasn't her type. She couldn't imagine that he was anybody's type. Washing down her aversion with a sip of Mexican beer, she turned her attention back to the bartender.

When Cascadia entered the cantina, there was an immediate inhalation of the stale air as every man looked up then held his breath. Each one of them appeared shocked as if he'd grabbed hold of an electric wire. Only Willy Nelson on the juke box seemed impervious as he sang mournfully on. Shaylee guessed that Spider saw an image of Cascadia that wiggled right off a girly calendar in some chop shop. Probably a babe in a wet tank top and precious little else. That's as far down that road as her imagination wanted to take her.

Cascadia walked to the vacant bar stool next to Shaylee and sat. Whatever they were seeing, men finger combed their hair, straightened their backs, sucked in their guts. But the only one to make a move was Spider. None of the others challenged his territorial imperative.

"Shaylee," he said, approaching the bar. "Nice to see you." But his eyes were on the spirit.

"Been a while, Spider." Shaylee tried to keep the nerves out of her voice which was threatening to rise an octave or two.

"You've been working a different part of the woods from my crews."

"Different kind of business, Spider."

"Who's your friend?" He turned full toward Cascadia.

"This is Lucita. She doesn't speak English."

"With looks like that, she doesn't have to speak anything. Going to introduce us?"

"I think not, Spider. You have your own crew. Lucita's working for me."

His gaze never left the spirit, but he spoke to Shaylee. "You don't run pickers."

"No. But Harley Waldon hired me to clear the dead wood out of that acreage he owns north of town. Going to create new view lots out there. I thought I'd have Lucita harvest some of the salal before I bring out the horses. It's easy pickings right now; the bushes I saw are at least five feet high. She'll be out there working Monday afternoon."

"Lot of territory for a girl on her own."

"That's why I chose a young and strong one."

"When she's done working for you, send her my way. I always need good workers."

Sure thing, jerk wad.

"Thanks, Spider. But she's joining a crew out near Mossy Rock later this week. Monday's the only day I'll have her clearing my job."

* * *

"It doesn't matter what they see. You aren't bound by it. Your interest is only in the one you hunt." Helen of Troy's coaching was audible only in the spirit's head. Cascadia listened to it as the wave of male desire washed over her when she entered the Cantina door and walked to Shaylee at the bar. Lust was as palpable to the spirit as the temperature in the room. Mostly it felt healthy and natural, like the desire she'd felt from Jim Bowie. Some of it even bordered on protective. Was that Jack projecting such concern? It was kind of, kind of ...

"Kind of sweet," said Helen in her mind. "You'll learn about being sweet some day. But probably not from me."

One man didn't project any desire for her at all. It confused Cascadia and made her worry she was doing something wrong. Once again, Helen came to her rescue. "That one would respond to Jim Bowie more than you, honey. Nothing to worry about."

But something else felt wrong. Very wrong. She concentrated on the human called Spider as he stood next to Shaylee but stared only at her. She had seen him before. In all the room, only he projected danger. And he was the only one she was here to show interest in. Even without looking down at her body, Cascadia could feel the rope marks on her wrists and the aching bruises, plus the puffy split lip that he imagined on her mouth.

She could tell Spider had nothing in mind but pleasure in her pain. It had been the same with the woman she had watched him murder out in the forest. He had a total void of compassion for any person ensnared in his web.

Was this it? The glitch in the human species that First Female failed to understand? Was it lust without compassion? A healthy fruit turned fetid? Or was there more to it?

An emotion with no moderation. She was too new to get it. But this was a clue, a place to begin. "It's just Mission One, kiddo," Helen said to comfort her. "You're not prepared to understand all the ways of humans yet. But you're prepared to stop this one."

Cascadia recalled her final order from First Female. "When you find the fault, cure it or end it." She would be the fixer First Female sought. She would start with this man. From what she'd seen him do, from the pain she felt when he looked at her, she realized a human could be a monster.

* * *

Monday morning the rain gave up and took the sullen sky with it, leaving the forest sunny and refreshed. A rejoicing chorus of woodland birds accompanied the horse loggers as they unloaded the day's equipment. Shaylee, Jack and Jamie were working a property remote from the spot where Cascadia and Silver Tip would be that afternoon.

"We can't just leave her out there alone," Jack griped to Shaylee. He'd been picking at it all morning like a dog worrying a bone. She'd tried to keep her patience but it was tough because she was worried, too. Finally, she burst like a balloon.

"She isn't alone, Jack! The bear is with her."

"The bear? What the fuck are you talking about? She's just a little Swedish girl who's caught the eye of, you'll pardon my French, a man with pig shit for morals."

A little Swedish girl?

Shaylee bit her lip, trying to repress her desire to blurt it all out. "Jack, I can't go. I promised I wouldn't."

"You promised who? *Who* doesn't want us there?" His ears and nose were turning red, this time from annoyance instead of booze. His mustache pumped up and down as he clenched his teeth.

Finally, her resistance crumbled. Counting on her fingers she snapped, "All three of them. Cascadia and Helen of Troy and First Female."

"Shaylee Ward, lie if you must, but don't make fun of me." He stomped away, heading uphill toward more trees to fell.

Shaylee sighed then opened the horse trailer doors. She felt bad enough about Cascadia, and now Jack had made it even worse. But what could she do? During the night, First Female's voice had come to her and told her, no *ordered* her, to stay away. "Presences may muck about with humans, not the other way around." Shaylee had been called on to set up the enemy, nothing more. This was Cascadia's fight now.

What can I do?

She unloaded the horses with Jamie's help. Together they harnessed Ghost and Gabrielle. Blue and Violet would work in the afternoon. Shaylee made several trips up the hillside to grapple the logs and pull them down to the landing site for Jamie to buck. Jack refused to say another word to her.

His sulking pissed her off, but it made her think it through again. Who knew just how vengeful First Female might be if she disobeyed? She'd said it could get dangerous when she first enlisted Shaylee, hadn't she? Surely First Female meant that Shaylee should stay involved or she wouldn't have warned of potential peril. Maybe she was just testing Shaylee, seeing if she'd take the easy way out. Cascadia was new and untried. Naive. She could get in real trouble.

Dammit all, why can't gods be clear about what they want? I have to go. I have to.

Shaylee told Jamie to harness Blue and Violet in order to let the two grays rest. He was to take the fresh team up the hill to Jack and grapple his first load on his own.

"You're putting me in charge of the horses this afternoon?" Jamie's young face lit up with delight.

"You're up to it, don't you think?" It was a hill the horses knew and a pull that was not too hard. If it had been a more demanding spot, she wouldn't have left the kid alone.

Probably.

"Sure am, boss."

"Good. I'll see you when you come back down." Shaylee waved him away.

As soon as he and the team were out of ear-shot, she trotted to Jack's battered Bronco and clambered up the high step to get in. The ancient SUV smelled of cherry pipe smoke and alcohol. She noticed the shotgun cradled in a steel rack hooked over the back seat. As she had figured, the keys were in the ignition; auto theft wasn't much of an issue this far back in the woods. After several tries that nearly flooded the time-worn engine, it turned over. Shaylee managed to find first gear.

Jack would be furious. He and Jamie would come down the hill for lunch. They wouldn't see her, probably call out for her. Then they'd notice Jack's Bronco was missing. He'd want to follow in her pickup, but Jamie wouldn't leave the horses behind. So they'd have to load the whole rig before coming after her. Jamie would miss his lunch, which would break his young heart.

By then she'd be long gone.

CHAPTER SIX

"Something for First Female to learn about humans is that we break our promises," Shaylee muttered as she floored the old Bronco. It fishtailed off the logging road and onto the black top, spitting gravel as she raced on her way. But First Female had a surprise for her. At least Shaylee blamed her for the enormous screw that flattened a rear tire and nearly blew her sideways off the road.

"Are you worried I'll get in Cascadia's way?" she asked as she dug out the jack.

"Do you think I'm just a talentless dope of a human ... one who'll screw things up?" she snapped while loosening the lug nuts.

"Do you even exist or am I imagining this whole damn thing?" She yelled while positioning the spare.

Then the truth of it hit her. "You think I can't be accused of a crime if I'm not at the crime scene. Of course! You're protecting me!" Shaylee's anger with the Presence drained away, but that left all the more room for dread. Changing the flat took forever. She tried not to think it, but she knew: she might not get there in time.

***

Cascadia, hidden high in a cedar tree, heard Spider thrashing through the underbrush, swearing at the blackberry bushes that snatched his pant legs. He made no effort at stealth. When he got where she could see him through the boughs above his head, she could smell his sweat and hear his heavy breathing. He might run crews of pickers, but he was no strenuous hiker himself.

As Spider passed below her, she turned to the pileated woodpecker beside her. "Now, Hammer," she whispered.

He cawed and rat-a-tatted in full voice. It was as raucous as a bird could get. Silver Tip would hear the warning cry, and he would get ready.

Then Cascadia energized her invisibility as she climbed down from her perch and cut through the trees to get in front of Spider. There was a small opening in the woods ahead, one where salal grew in profusion.

Cascadia never for a second thought that she might lose the coming battle. Helen of Troy had told her that spirits and goddesses often failed in mythologies from around the world. But she had no concept that it could happen to her. Cascadia placed herself in front of the salal bushes and dropped her invisible guard so the man would see her. Then she began picking.

To make extra noise to lead him toward her, she sang the Willy Nelson song about being crazy, the one she remembered hearing in Cappy's Cantina.

Spider came nearer. Cascadia sang louder.

She smelled him but gave no reaction as she harvested. She was drawing him close enough to put Bowie's lessons to the test, to slide the knife between his ribs for an efficient kill.

She waited a breath too long.

"So you do speak English," Spider snarled as he swung the machete at her. "I'll enjoy your begging all the more."

She turned in time for the flat side of the tool to catch her shoulder instead of her head. Pain erupted and she staggered back, but she aimed a kick at his crotch. She connected but was too far away for full force.

Spider grunted, grabbed her raised foot and tipped her backwards to the ground. He dropped to his knees between her legs, forcing them apart. When he leaned over her, she was pinned by his full weight.

"A fighter, huh? Here's what happens to pushy bitches."

She'd underestimated the strength of a human male. His speed, his strength amazed her. He bit her breasts and cuffed her head until black spots clouded her vision. He felt enormous as she fought to reach her knife. But he got to it first.

"Let's just see what we can do with this pretty little blade." His spittle speckled her face like a predator drooling over its prey. With one massive hand around her neck to pin her in place, he lifted himself up and began dragging the knife slowly from her chest toward her pubis. "I find a knife helps a reluctant little gal to settle right down." The knife sliced through the silk of the dress that he fantasized, peeling it back like the petals of a flower. The blade left a thin red line between her breasts and down her stomach as it travelled over her skin.

Cascadia wrestled as he inched the blade toward her vagina, trickles of blood now seeping along her body. She could not throw him no matter how she writhed. He laughed at her, and his breath smelled of rot. For the first time, she understood the terror and desperation of human women confronted by such power. Shaylee and Helen had both told her that lust could be about domination. Nothing here was like lust with Jim Bowie. Or the West Wind. This was torture. She had thought she could fight it off. But not without help.

She called out for Silver Tip.

Several things happened almost at once.

First, the furious grizzly thrashed across the meadow. Silver Tip stopped directly behind the human and growled mightily into his ear. Those massive drooling jaws froze Spider in place.

"Steady," Cascadia crooned to the bear. "Get off me, human."

Spider remained where he was. He pleaded, "If I move, he'll kill me."

"Not unless I let him."

Next, Shaylee appeared through the trees, pumping a shell into Jack's old shotgun. "You heard her, Spider. Get off her!" The click, click pump of the gun seemed to terrify Spider as much as the bear. At least the beast was under order to stay.

"Careful with that thing, Shaylee," he said as he moved slowly away, out of his crouch. But in a swift swing of his arm, he threw Cascadia's beautiful knife straight at Shaylee's heart. The flying death raced true toward its target. It stopped a hair's breadth short, hovered there briefly, then arched back to Cascadia's control like a magical boomerang.

That's when Helen of Troy appeared, mincing across the meadow in her strappy sandals.

Shaylee and Spider both looked stunned by this visitation from the pantheon of time, but Cascadia scrambled up and took over.

"Silver Tip, back away," she said, knife now in her hand. She pressed it firmly against Spider's spider tattoo then she tapped the bear's snout with a finger. He huffed at her, curled his lip, then acted. A bear, even a good bear, has to exercise a little authority now and then.

Silver Tip bit off the man's ear before backing away. He returned to the woods, munching on his treat. It was a tiny morsel for the bear, but an excruciating loss for the man.

Over Spider's shrieks, Shaylee asked of everyone or anyone, "Did you all see that? The knife! It stopped! Why didn't it kill me?"

"Because, darling," cooed Helen. "First Female improved Mr. Bowie's knife with a little magic of her own. It can kill any human being. Except you."

Shaylee expelled a huge breath, then nodded. "Excellent modification to the original design."

Cascadia poked the knife tip into the center of Spider's tattoo to get his attention. He'd been preoccupied with the bleeding gap where an ear had been.

"Stop sniveling. And tell me now. Why do you attack women?"

Maybe his pain was too excessive for him to heed what he said. Maybe he didn't believe a woman would really kill him. Or maybe he was too screwed up to feel real fear. Pure hatred spit the words at her. "Women aren't good for shit except a fuck."

"And to you, fucking means fear and pain?"

"All men would agree if they had the balls. Bitches gotta be kept in line. Otherwise, you're nothing but –"

Shaylee cut him off. "He's sick, Cascadia. Disgusting but sick. He can't show remorse. He doesn't know how. We need to call the law now."

Spider rushed to agree. "That's right, Shaylee. Stop this. People saw us together at the bar. They'll come to you with questions if I disappear. Stop this now and we can all just walk away."

But there was no stopping Helen of Troy. She pushed Shaylee and Cascadia aside. "I was raped by men like you when I was just a child. I was defenseless. Not so much anymore, though." Helen hit him full in the face. Her gold and opal ring left an impressive gash.

Spider made a move for her, but the spirit had heard enough. As he lunged at the goddess, Cascadia sliced through his jugular. His neck opened in a wide jester's smile with the white of bone visible beneath. She made the thrust just as Jim Bowie had taught her. She could hear her Skill Master cheering in the wind.

The mutilated body that fell at her feet didn't look

so fearsome now. "Come, Cassie," Helen said. "Let us go treat your cuts." And then they were gone.

* * *

Shaylee called Jack and Jamie when she was back in cell range to tell them it was over. They met at Rainbow Café in town, midway between their two locations.

"What happened?" Jack asked, sitting in a booth across from Shaylee and Jamie. All three had steaming mugs of coffee. The café had no liquor license.

"I have nothing to report," Shaylee said.

"But where is she, the little Swedish girl? Is she safe?"

"She's safe. And she's gone, Jack. But she asked me to give this to you and thank you for thinking of her as worthy of your protection." She handed him a key ring with a Swedish troll doll, modeled on those popular in the 60s. But this one was made of the purest gold. "She says it's good luck."

Jack stared at the silly little treasure. "Where on earth did she get this?"

Not on earth at all.

"No idea, Jack. Just accept that the woods are safer for women than they were a day ago."

Jamie asked, "Is anyone ordering something to eat?"

* * *

It was half time during the Northern Lights show. Old Man Above stretched then scratched himself. Slowly he realized it had been some time since he'd chatted with First Female.

74

"How's it going with that little spirit of yours, my enchantress?"

First Female, humming her favorite tune about a sorcerer's apprentice, was busy messing with Shaylee's memory cells. By now a cloud would be forming in the human's grey matter. She would be unsure of every detail, how much was dream or reality. It would keep her from talking about it lest other humans doubt her sanity. But Shaylee Ward would be easy to reenlist when Cascadia had need of her again.

"Little spirit of mine? She's just fine, dear."

"I'll bet she is. That Helen could teach hot to a forest fire ... er, but not as well as *you* could, my heart."

First Female glanced sideways at him but let it pass. "The spirit is new at this, but did well in her first trial and will do better in those to come. She has discovered that a lack of compassion may be the missing link in some human make-up."

She put a final touch to Shaylee's brain, one that would allow her a rewarding night's sleep. She owed this human that much, even though she did not accept something Shaylee had said to Cascadia. "It is true Spider was cruel," Shaylee had said. "But you didn't need to kill him. Human life has value. Even his."

How strange humans are to think such thoughts.

"Some humans believe evil can be defeated," First Female said to Old Man Above who may even have been listening. "They value life more than we do. That's a mystery for us to explore further."

"Or maybe we will have to convince them they are wrong," Old Man Above said before grabbing another handful of Caldera Crunch.

First Female said, "Either way, Cascadia and Shaylee will soon meet again. But first, the spirit must train with another goddess and human ancient."

The lights sparkled back to life, electrifying the sky with inconceivable color. "Hush now, my eternal love," said Old Man Above. "The rest of the game is about to begin."

PART TWO

Wherein evildoers discover it is never wise to irritate
a magic bear
and Shaylee spends quality time
with a lust partner

CHAPTER SEVEN

Old Man Above was in a snit. He sighed mightily, producing a gust of wind that pounded the coast with rogue waves.

"Whatever is the matter?" First Female asked looking up from the basin she was dredging on the north face of Storm King Mountain.

"Have you seen their most recent butchery? What they're doing to my bears? What, for the love of me, are the humans up to this time?"

Old Man Above was not the sort to dwell on causes. But, damnation. Were human failings his fault? Maybe he'd made life too hard on them. But humans should pay for the extraordinary gifts they'd been given, shouldn't they? He was blindsided by how many of the rascals, when under stress, turned on their own kind. And even crazier, on their own environment.

It especially yanked his chain when they misbehaved in Cascadia. Of all the places he'd created - with the help of First Female, of course, and goddess forbid he ever forget that - *this* was his favorite. These mountains and forests, these waters and this wildlife. This was the culmination of his creation art. What, then, was wrong with the humans?

"Maybe I've gone too far with the *struggle* bit. Tested them too hard."

First Female rejoined, "Of course you've gone too far, my dear. You have no natural talent for moderation. Life is exceedingly difficult for many of them these days."

She was right, of course, based on recent behavior. Earlier humans had honored Cascadia; now they plundered it. His living creations - plants and animals - were being slaughtered by the thousands. Now even his bears.

He frowned, and the skies eclipsed the earth momentarily with terrifying darkness. "That little spirit we created, the one named for Cascadia," he said.

"*We* created?" First Female was holding her new lake, ready to place it in the mountain basin.

"I have a project for her. But only if you agree, my enchantress." He caught himself in time, remembering to ask politely. He explained what he had in mind.

"Hmmm. Yes. Crimes against nature would fit nicely with her next stage of development," First Female said as she allowed the water to tumble earthward. Distracted by the sound she said, "*Tum-tum* is the word our first people used for waterfall, and I quite like the sound of it. Tum, tum. Like water smacking down on rocks. Humans can be quite imaginative."

"So you'll help?" Old Man Above asked, biting down on his impatience.

"Yes. Yes, I will. Cascadia now knows human evil exists and that her mission is to cure it or end it. It would strengthen her resolve if she had even more that our command to obey. She needs to be personally involved to truly avenge or revenge. Yes. She could use the emotion of Outrage." She smiled at Old Man Above. "I know who can help with that."

To him, her smile was always as warm as a second sun. Nonetheless, he shivered. Old Man Above knew who First Female had in mind. And the presence of the Daughter of Darkness always meant someone or something was about to be judged harshly.

"We have any more of that Caldera Crunch?" He asked. "I have a bad taste in my mouth."

* * *

Silver Tip had been given the gift of flight by Old Man Above and First Female. In return, he was tasked with taking care of Cascadia. But on this lovely sunny day, she was taking care of him.

Cascadia was humanoid in shape but not terribly tall so her chin was about the same height as the humped shoulders of the bear. He turned his great head toward her, lifted his paw and whined pitifully. His black beady eyes looked so sad that she'd swear she could see tears forming.

"You are a big baby," she said. Then she scratched that spot between his ears that brought him such joy. "But you are *my* big baby, and Hammer says that the human who lives in this cabin can help you."

The bear had sliced his paw on a broken bottle in a creek. From its color and label, Cascadia recognized it as having once contained the amber liquid that humans called beer. She'd smelled it on the breath of men at Cappy's Cantina, a dangerous place she'd visited once upon a time with her familiar, Shaylee Ward.

Cascadia had removed the large shard of glass that sliced through the paw's tough pad, and she cleaned the area. Nonetheless, smaller fragments could still be embedded under the skin, and she had no knowledge of healing.

She had consulted Hammer, the pileated woodpecker who lived near the Tree of Human History, a thousand-year-old Western cedar. The bird was a busybody, a gossip who knew it all. His rat-a-tat-tat from tree to tree was the forest telegraph for those who could interpret it. First Female had provided Cascadia with such a language skill.

Silver Tip whined again, then licked the bloody slit on the pad of his forepaw. Together he and Cascadia approached the cabin. The logs that created it fit together tightly, and the roof of hand split shingles had just enough of a pitch to repel snow. River stones at the corners and along the sills could keep out the damp, and solar panels in the roof no doubt provided hot water and heat. The person who lived here enjoyed comfort. According to Hammer, that person was a medicine woman, an herbalist. Maybe even a witch. Humans sought out her unguents and poultices for heartache to heartburn and everything in between.

"Surely she will have something to help a needy bear," Cascadia said to Silver Tip. He whimpered yet again.

As they neared the cabin, a blast of buckshot whizzed over their heads. "Get down," Cascadia yelled as she removed her Bowie knife from its white leather sheath. Silver Tip snarled but dropped to the ground next to her, behind a pile of field boulders.

Cascadia peeked around the rocks at the cabin, and saw a woman standing on its deck, shotgun at the ready. The spirit could easily have hit the human with a throw of her deadly knife or at the very least, donned invisibility. But she needed this human's help. So she stood again in plain sight, an easy target. "I ask you to put the gun down. I mean you no harm."

"Yeah? Well, what about the griz? Who comes calling with a thing like that at her side?"

"My name is Cascadia."

"Oh, crap. You're that concoction of First Female's, aren't you? Come to save human kind." The old woman rolled her eyes but set the gun down, leaning it against the cabin wall. "Now don't go tattling to her that I tried to kill you. If I'd meant to, I would have."

"I would not tattle." That was true enough. Cascadia had no intention of being a tattletale like Hammer. When he'd told the entire forest about her lusting with Jim Bowie, she'd suffered an unpleasant feeling, one that made her cheeks hot and her stomach clench. One snitch in the forest was quite enough.

The woman squinted. "Come closer so I can see you clearly. And keep that monster of yours under control. There ought to be leash laws around here."

Cascadia walked to the cabin porch and stopped. She was wary, not yet trusting this gunslinger. Silver Tip grumbled his displeasure as he limped his way forward along with her.

Close up, she could tell the woman had seen many seasons but was not yet an ancient. Her skin looked leathery from sun damage more than old age. Her hair, pulled back in a careless knot, still had plenty of dark blonde amidst the gray. She was tall but hunched forward as though her heavy breasts were too much for her shoulders to hold up any more. Cascadia thought the woman could use the help of a corset like the one Jim Bowie had envisioned.

The spirit did not recognize what human group this one was from. She was more brown than white, more statuesque than squatty. One eye was hazel, the other blue. At least two front teeth were missing so her voice had a soft whistle when she spoke.

The woman appeared to examine Cascadia as closely as the other way around and then pronounced, "Well, First Female didn't do you any favors in the looks department. You're damn ordinary, sister." She cocked her head and smiled. "'Course, I'm no looker myself. Let's start over. My name is Aiyanna. It means *ever blooming*. Guess I'll be pushing up daisies even after I leave the topside of this earth."

Cascadia nodded. "You are the one Hammer sent me to see. This bear is Silver Tip. His paw has been injured, and I do not know what to do. Can you help him?" Cascadia was skeptical although she didn't know the word. So far, this woman struck her as addled even by human standards. But she had to hope for a cure.

"Might can do. Can you hold him still?"

"That won't be necessary." Cascadia stared a silent communication to the bear. In his own good time, Silver Tip lowered his ample bottom to the ground then rolled onto his back, presenting the pad of his forepaw to the two women. In the process he trumpeted a fart that rivaled Hammer in volume.

"This is why I rarely ask a bear to tip over," Aiyanna said, fanning the air in front of her nose as her eyes watered. Then she straightened her glasses. They were taped together in the center, and looked no better aligned when she was done fussing with them. While Cascadia watched intently, the healer clutched the four-inch claws on the bear's paw to turn it toward the sunlight. She set her face in a frown that made her look like a dried carved apple. She peered at the paw. She squeezed it. She tsk-tsked over it. Then she let go and said to Cascadia, "That's a paw, all right. I'll be back shortly."

While they waited for the healer to return from the cabin, Cascadia thanked Silver Tip for not raking the woman wide open with his claws. She promised she'd pick him four handfuls of huckleberries after the medical procedure was done.

Aiyanna came back carrying a wooden bowl filled with water, a ball of soap, a pile of rags, and a battered shoe polish can. She unpinned a needle from her chambray shirt and sterilized it with a kitchen match. Grabbing the paw once more, she removed several tiny glass splinters with the needle, then washed the area with the soap ball.

"I make it from fat and things I find on the forest floor plus a dash of magic. It's antiseptic for my hands and his paw." The old woman spoke softly as she worked, her voice becoming less grating and more comforting.

Aiyanna heated the needle again then threaded it with fish line. "Don't think I have anything else to hold skin this tough." She sewed the cut together. Cascadia could tell this healer had been mending wounds since long before her own creation. She began to trust. Silver Tip, after a snivel, began to relax.

Aiyanna twisted the lid off the shoe polish can and revealed an odiferous dark brown sludge. Even Silver Tip wrinkled his nose. "Nobody said a paste of arnica, cayenne pepper and Saint John's Wort smelled good, big boy. But you're no picnic neither." She smeared a lump of the goo onto the wound and massaged Silver Tip's paw until the paste melted between the stitches deep into the wound. She then wrapped it with a dressing of rags.

"How's that?" she said patting the paw as she released it.

Silver Tip sniffed at the bandage, shook the paw, then stood. He gingerly put weight on it. He snorted a mighty blow.

"He feels better!" exclaimed Cascadia. The effervescent gladness she felt was delight. "I owe you, Aiyanna."

The old woman laughed. "I'm pretty sure you spirits don't go around with cash."

"I have this," Cascadia said, detaching a pouch from her belt and handing it over.

Aiyanna opened it. A twist of bright gold fell into her hand. The bracelet's intricate pattern of vines supported a clasp of inlaid pearls and carnelian. The healer's mismatched eyes sparkled with amazement when she looked up at Cascadia and handed the bracelet back. "You keep this safe, sister. It's worth a fortune. Where on earth did you get it?"

"It was given to me by Helen of Troy."

* * *

As the days of summer passed, Silver Tip healed and Aiyanna became an important human to Cascadia. If spirits had mothers, she would have chosen this woman for hers. As surely as tree leaves cycle through stages, trust grew into affection, and affection blossomed into caring. It teetered dangerously close to love, although that was such a complex human emotion that Cascadia did not yet understand it.

"Neither do most humans," Aiyanna said when the spirit asked about it. "Ask your familiar."

The healer was a human both older and wiser than Cascadia's familiar, Shaylee Ward. Shaylee was her strategic partner and a warrior in her own right. With Aiyanna, Cascadia was a student, quietly absorbing the healer's strength. Cascadia now had two humans who convinced her of the species' inherent goodness.

How could such excellent creatures go so very wrong?

First Female watched this relationship with Aiyana as it developed. She exchanged a sad smile with Old Man Above. They both knew the truth of it. It was time for Cascadia to learn about the outrage that could be created by loss of love.

* * *

Cascadia spent most of the day in the embrace of Dogoda, the gentle Slavic spirit of the West Wind. She craved his loving touch, dancing in the air as leaves swirled all about them. The two were destined to meet only when the colors rose both in the trees and in Cascadia's lithe body. These colors that warmed her within were the gift of Helen of Troy. They made her flights with Dogoda more exciting than ever before. But Dogoda, bittersweet and fleeting as his season, was destined to be on his way.

Now it was near dark, just past dusk when eyesight is losing its power. Cascadia flew to her favorite pool aboard the back of a much improved Silver Tip. Her sorrow over the departure of Dogoda was overshadowed by the grizzly's joy. He pranced and bounded through the air as frisky as Pegasus. The stitches had been removed, and his paw had healed with a bad ass scar he was quite proud of.

They didn't see it coming.

From nowhere, a great beating of wings assaulted their ears, along with painful shrieks far more terrible than any earth bird's cries. Three identical beasts emerged from obscurity, a nightmare come to life. Their heads were enormous eagles, but their bodies were long muscled lions ready to pounce and slash with vicious raptor talons.

Silver Tip reared in the air to his full nine foot height and released a war cry even louder than the shrieks of the mystery beasts. Lesser forest animals ran and hid. In the same instant, Cascadia unsheathed her knife, set to accompany her flying bear into battle.

87

"Cease!" demanded a voice, cutting through all the animal threats. "My three griffins against your one bear? It is not fair." The three mythological beasts stopped in space, their great wings arched as they rode the wind. Their bird-like screams were replaced by the hissing of wild cats.

"Show yourself," Cascadia demanded of the voice she had heard. She followed with a taunt. "Three bird-cats will lose to one war bear every time." She was pretty sure that was true.

As if they were one, the griffins rotated to the side. Cascadia could now see that they pulled an ink-dark chariot. A figure stood tall within, but it was too dark to see her clearly.

"Oh, cease your nincompoopery. Put away Jim Bowie's knife and lower yourselves to ground. We shall land as well. I come to you from First Female."

Another goddess from the boss meant another foray was about to begin. Cascadia's belligerence became giddy expectation.

But nincompoopery? What the hell is that?

Cascadia had learned lust and she liked it rather a lot, so she was eager to try another human emotion. She tapped the bear between the ears with the palm of her hand. After a series of huffs and blows, Silver Tip responded to her command. He dropped gently to the meadow beside the pool, and Cascadia slid down from his back. Together they watched the chariot descend.

The griffins came down in a graceful spiral, the ebony chariot following to a soft landing. Its rider was still cloaked in darkness, but Cascadia began to see a goddess in a chiton far plainer than any dress Helen of Troy ever wore. Her only adornment was a golden crown. Maybe it was a shadow from this headpiece that made her face so mysterious. Or it was the tone of the skin. No, not that. Not race, not complexion. It was a gloom that moved with the goddess as if a dark mood had become visible.

The rider held in her hand a whip with many lashes. She stepped regally down from the chariot and towered over Cascadia. The spirit would never disrespect a goddess, even one as distant and cold as a dark star, so she spoke with reverence. "I am Cascadia. I welcome you here."

"My name is Nemesis. Humans have also called me the Daughter of Night, the Spirit of Retribution, the Punisher." The goddess shrugged. "Humans do not like me very much."

Cascadia was inclined to side with the humans. Nemesis was spooky, her face hidden by a shadowy black gauze. "Why is your face veiled? I cannot see your eyes, goddess."

"Nor shall you. I am the daughter of Nyx, goddess of the night. As it did with my mother, this dark mist haunts me from the underworld, blotting out most light. My vision is weak, therefore I see you as poorly as you see me. It is fair that it be so."

"That is the second time you have mentioned fairness." Cascadia knew the concept because she had learned to share equally with her bear.

"You are observant, new one. This pleases me. You will soon find that equanimity is my only guide."

"You have come from the Chamber of Mythologies to teach me another emotion?" Cascadia had no guile with which to hide her excitement.

A taut smile appeared on the cold face of Nemesis. "I see Helen of Troy's lessons pleased you. My subject is less agreeable than hers. As I am less agreeable than she. Some say I'm her mother."

Cascadia couldn't believe it. Surely this icy presence could not have birthed the hot-blooded Helen.

While spirit and goddess talked, the three griffins preened and cleaned as bird-cats will do. To Cascadia they smelled of sweat in the manner of working teams. Silver Tip put one of his massive paws over his nose, rumbling a noise that in bear language was less than kind. One of the creatures licked his mighty talons then rubbed his own face. Another lifted his leonine tail in the air and cleaned his ass. The third commenced to pluck and fluff her chest with her beak. Eventually, like cats everywhere, they curled in a pile of togetherness to suck up the most possible body warmth. Unlike most cats, the griffins spread their great wings over themselves, locking them together in a protective feathered blanket. The whole pile of animal vibrated with a mighty purr.

Silver Tip watched in disgust, then turned his back. He meandered to the trees that rimmed the meadow and bedded down out of the vicinity of the half-breeds. But he kept his eyes on Cascadia in case she had need of him. He was not fond of Helen, the first goddess he had met. Why should this taller, icier one be any different?

Before Cascadia joined Silver Tip to rest against his warm thick fur, she listened to the story that Nemesis told by light of the Milky Way.

"I've been saddled with more names than most, as you already know. Mesomedes, that sanctimonious poet from Crete, dubbed me 'Nemesis, winged balancer of life, dark-faced goddess, daughter of Justice.' It's not really fair, all this name-calling. I was fated to be the adjudicator of mankind and had no choice in the matter. I cannot abide injustice. I avenge crime and destroy hurtful pride."

Cascadia knit her brows. "I do not understand. That all seems *good* for humans to me."

Nemesis agreed. "Yes, well, some say I go too far, that I smite too aggressively. Sometimes doing a job well means angering the populace. I'm not a diplomat, you know. I'm a judge. Everything must be balanced in my view. A human can't be too happy or I will bring her suffering. Wealth must come with loss. I provide retribution for undeserved good fortune. I am the reason that the human condition will always include grief."

Cascadia blinked. "I begin to see why you can be difficult to like."

"You've noticed the whip I carry?" Nemesis held up the many-lashed exhibit. "It is not merely a symbol. I've used it. Both this scourge and I are called the Punisher."

Cascadia repressed a shudder. "Helen taught me how to use a human's desire. What are you here to teach?"

"What I teach you will hurt."

"Hurt how? Why?" Cascadia thought this goddess was getting harder to like all the time.

"Outrage is the emotion you will learn from me. Not only will it hurt, but I must warn you of another potential result of your outrage."

"What result?"

"You will lose your innocence if you become judgmental. You, too, could become known as a punisher. You would end up alone."

* * *

Cascadia fretted through the night. Even the nearness of her bear could not comfort her. She did not understand this presence that First Female had sent. Of course, she had not understood Helen of Troy either, and they had become as close as a spirit and a goddess could be. Maybe all would be well. "In goddess we trust, right?" she muttered to the sleeping bear.

In the morning, much to Silver Tip's disapproval, Cascadia ordered him to stay while she joined Nemesis in the chariot. He didn't understand the language of the griffins, but he was sure they were laughing at him as they swiftly carried the goddess and the spirit away. He no longer remembered how he lived his life before Cascadia entered it. He was bereft without her. Well, except now there might be time to harvest the wild blackberries. Or a tasty salmon. Maybe a little time alone wouldn't be so bad.

Cascadia flew with Nemesis to the coast where they hovered over a human village. A great ocean glimmered to the west. The three griffins kept watch on the land to the north, east and south. "We are undetectable to human eyes now, appearing only as a brief shadow crossing between their dwellings and the sun," the goddess explained.

The sky seemed darker to Cascadia just being this close to Nemesis.

"To humans, evil in others is often invisible. They don't recognize impending doom. Most of them are simply too optimistic or kind." Nemesis shook her head. "Such naiveté is hard to fathom."

"Kindness is not a good thing?" Cascadia was confused again. Aiyanna and Shaylee both seemed kind to her.

"Let me show you what I mean. See that building with children playing in the yard?" As they observed from above, a bell rang and the grade schoolers ran back inside while a teacher rounded up the stragglers and shooed them along. "The picture of innocence, yes? Nobody would suspect that two of the children are carrying loaded guns."

The griffins next hovered over a main street, floating like a menacing Macy's Parade balloon. "The people with animals going into that office? They think the veterinarian will treat their companions with compassion. But he has been known to hurt them when their owners are not there to see. And that fellow over there directing traffic onto the ferry? He goes home and beats his wife."

Cascadia felt distress. Nemesis was so ... bleak. "This human stuff is confusing. How can they pick on each other so?"

"Kindness often blinds them to badness. Good humans fail to see it when it appears. This is why you,

93

Cascadia, must be more vigilant than they to the true nature of the people around them."

"But how can I recognize human evil that *humans* don't see?"

"That is the next part of the lesson. Outrage is your best weapon against evil. It overcomes your fear, doubt, incomprehension, even threatens your logic. Nothing will hold you back from doling out retribution."

With that, Nemesis called sharply to the griffins and they swept away, back to the meadow where Silver Tip awaited their return. He was munching on a salmon, his favorite comfort food. Cascadia joined him, but he offered her none of his catch. Bad-ass bears sulk when their feelings have been hurt.

The spirit sat in the groundcover and the Daughter of Darkness perched on the same boulder that Helen of Troy had favored as a throne for her lectures. "First Female provided invisibility. The elixir from Helen of Troy enables you to be desirable to any man. My gift will allow you to see into their hearts to know the truth about them." From a pocket hidden in her dreary chiton, Nemesis extracted a tiny ebony box decorated in gold filigree. She handed it to Cascadia. "Open this."

Removing the lid Cascadia revealed a ring on a velvet cushion. It was not the ornate jewelry of Helen of Troy, but a simple, sleek design with two united bands, one of iron and the other of sapphire.

"This is the Ring of Gyges," Nemesis said. "It grants the wearer invisibility. Plato used it two thousand years ago to prove any man will do injustice when nobody can see him do it. But it is not the invisibility that you need, Cascadia. It is the ring's second property that will open your eyes."

The goddess slipped the ring onto the middle finger of Cascadia's left hand. The metal felt cold and its considerable weight was foreign. Nemesis said, "Unknown to all at the time, this ring has a second magical power. It gives you access to the human soul. Come close."

Cascadia leaned forward and the goddess spoke so softly that neither the bear nor the bird-cats could hear even if they hadn't been fighting over fish bones. After a moment, Nemesis leaned back. In her full bleak voice she said, "The ring will act when you put your lips against it and whisper those words. It will grow even colder, and the sapphire will shimmer like blue ice when it detects human evil."

Cascadia gazed at the ring, eager to try it out, but there was not a human anywhere around.

"Listen to my warnings, spirit. First, you must never reveal the secret words. If you do, the ring will become the property of an evil one. He or she will be invisible at will. And second." Nemesis stopped and sighed. "Now that I have given you a gift, I am bound to take one away. That is the nature of equilibrium."

Cascadia looked at the goddess with curiosity. Just what did she have to part with? The bracelet from Helen of Troy? Her knife from Jim Bowie? She began to worry when she realized how much the things she'd been given now mattered to her.

"You must suffer the threat of personal loss to experience outrage at its fullest. And, little one, there is no greater loss than love. Love is an emotion that many of us in the Chamber of Mythology envy. Humans have far more of it than we do. They can be very loving and lovable. You are developing affection for them, are you not?"

Cascadia smiled at the thought of Shaylee and Aiyanna, but the next words from Nemesis chilled to the bone.

"How would you feel if you were to lose one of them at the hands of other humans?" On the surface of the still pool, Nemesis projected a vision. Cascadia saw a senseless mob armed with torches burning Aiyanna as a witch for practicing black arts. She cried out in alarm. "Stop them!"

Nemesis said, "That anger you feel – the acid in your stomach, the heat rising in your chest, the pounding in your head – that, my dear, is *outrage*."

The vision changed. Cascadia saw the uncle who had ravaged Shaylee when she was just a child. He appeared to be coming back for more. The spirit leaped up as the vision dissolved away, furious at the man and at the goddess for showing her this vile image.

"Stop this, goddess, or I will."

Silver Tip heard her cry and instantly gathered his enormous self to battle ready.

Fearing for their goddess, the griffins did the same.

"As you were, beasts of war," Nemesis commanded, with a threatening rise of her whip. At least for the moment, they listened. "Cascadia. Interpret your body now. Clenched fists, vision focused on your target, fast breathing, pounding heart. These, too, are the signs of outrage."

Cascadia was in pain. Outrage ached like a festering wound.

"I told you it would hurt. This is because I have taken from you the ability to love without fear of loss. That is payment for the ring. You will be on guard forever. Enemies are all around those beings that matter to you most. But for now, Aiyanna and Shaylee are safe."

"Let me punish the offenders if this is to be the future." Cascadia rose to full height and mounted her war bear.

"Listen, spirit. First Female chose me as your teacher of outrage for one important reason. I am the Goddess of Retribution. Be sure any punishment you deliver is no greater than the crime. Do not allow justice to become injustice."

Cascadia drew her knife. "I am ready when the time comes."

"A knife won't work well with more than one enemy," Nemesis said. "I will bring you a human who will teach you the astonishing capabilities of the Web of Revenge."

CHAPTER EIGHT

Antigonus was a killer. He'd cut the throats and punctured the eyes of more adversaries than he could count.

He was a Retiarius, the very lowest of the gladiator class from the second century A.D. Antigonus was allowed no armor other than an arm guard, brawling almost nude with only a net, trident and dagger. As an enslaved barbarian, he was expected to die at the hands of warriors. But time after time, he survived by his rapid body feints and quick wits. Men in helmets, masks and chest plates, protected with shields, came to fear him.

If he'd ever been a normal man, there was little normality left in Antigonus. Like a dog maltreated until it fights, he only knew how to battle on. He was consumed by outrage over the wrongs done to him. He was, therefore, surprised that Nemesis retrieved him out of time through a request to the Tree of Human History. He was not a member of that august body since nobody wanted to be near him, not ever. He knew nothing of other human legends while he suffered in the amphitheaters of Italy.

"But they know who and where you are," Nemesis explained to him after those on the Tree delivered him to her. "They only trust me to handle you because they consider me as much of a whack job as you. They don't want anything to do with either of us."

Antigonus barely allowed the Daughter of Darkness temporary dominion over him and then only because she was a patroness of gladiators. "You are among the few gods I respect," he growled. "Like me, you are vilified."

"It is for the sake of justice that you are here."

Antigonus scoffed. "Justice. I have never found it for myself. But if you command it, I will do my best to deliver it for you. Point me to your foe. When he is dead or dying here in this unknown arena of ferns, mosses and flowers, return me to the earth and time I know. There I must battle on."

"No foe here," Nemesis replied. "Your mission is not to retaliate but to teach."

"Shit of the Cyclops," he sneered in an ancient Roman oath. "What have I to teach except that humans are cruel even beyond the gods?"

"Silence, gladiator," she scolded, her aura darkening all the more. "The gods have provided you the greatest net skills of all time. It is that ability that you will teach, not your bitter beliefs." She softened then, enough that he could hear it in her voice. "You and I have both seen the worst of mankind from centuries long ago. But we cannot communicate our hopelessness to our young student."

She returned to the cold tone he preferred from her. She explained what was expected of him in order to prepare Cascadia for future battles. "Your teaching methods are your own. But, goddess willing, you will not injure your apprentice. And remember, she has a bear."

Antigonus had no idea what a bear was, but he'd defeated lions in his time. No beast scared him. However, when he saw Cascadia the very first time, he sucked in his breath. She had something far more dangerous to him than a bear. Just the sight of her compounded the impossible sorrow he'd had since the soldiers carried his daughter away. This girl looked as frail, as innocent as that child of his own.

He felt a prickle on the back of his neck and a bolt of fear so strong it pierced through the scar tissue of his heart. This was passion of a whole different sort, a fire to protect this young one. His was lust for life, to keep her safe. He couldn't lose her as he had his own child. The dreads of fatherhood reentered his soul, the terrible agony of a protector unable to save the one in his care. It nearly brought him to his knees.

Cascadia did this to him. And he was furious about it.

There she was, a fragile girl sitting beside a forest pool weaving a basket from split spruce. He could demolish her in a heartbeat. But if he hurt her at all, Nemesis would set the Furies loose on him. Antigonus had been damned by gods often enough in his life. He didn't need any more of that crap.

With resignation, he soundlessly unwound the net looped around his arm, took aim and tossed. It settled gently over Cascadia, and he pulled the draw string. As she jumped up, with the startled grace of a doe, the net slipped tighter. Her struggles for freedom entangled her all the more until she was encased like a fly in a web.

When Cascadia finally exhausted her efforts to escape, and lay gasping on the ground, Antigonus neared her. He poked her lightly on the shoulder with the trident he carried, not breaking the skin although the weapon easily could. Its three prongs were as sharp as a griffin's talons. He said, "This is where you say, 'We who are about to die salute you.'"

The pile of wrath trapped in the net spit at him. "And this is where you will be eaten if you poke me again."

Antigonus became aware of the rumble of thunder and hot wind blowing out of the forest and across the meadow.

Earthquake? Tornado? Volcano? No.

Bear.

* * *

Silver Tip charged at a speed that astounded even Cascadia. He halted protectively over her, a forepaw to each side, his huge head low and ready for his lunge. He awaited her command.

"I'll call him off if you release me," she snarled at her captor.

"I'll kill him if you don't." The gladiator raised the trident ready to throw.

Stand off. Tempers and blood pressure escalated until the air felt depleted of oxygen.

Cascadia knew she was awaiting a Skill Master, one Nemesis called a gladiator. But no teacher would be as brutish as this, would he? Or as ugly. He was nothing but a map of scrapes, wounds and

101

mutilations. Because he was clothed by little more than a loin cloth, she could see that beneath the scar tissue littering his entire being, his body was as lean and well-muscled as any stag in the forest.

Cascadia realized this new Skill Master had already taught her one thing. She could feel outrage for herself as well as for humans. She would not forget this humiliating lesson.

An ungodly shriek from the griffins sliced the tension between the warriors. Cascadia wished the Daughter of Darkness could make them quit that awful racket. Antigonus put his hands over his ears.

"Cease, all of you below!" commanded Nemesis. The chariot pushed the gladiator and spirit apart as it landed between them with a thud and a great flapping of wings. The goddess looked back and forth, pointing a judicial finger from one to the other. "You remove that net, and you stand down that bear. Do it now."

Grumbling, Antigonus loosened the drawstring so Cascadia could shed the rope mesh. Cascadia, with a silent command, made Silver Tip withdraw to the tree line where he kept a close watch, grumbling bear swear words to himself.

"That introduction went well," Nemesis said.

"I don't like her," Antigonus answered while wrapping the net around his arm.

"I don't like him," Cascadia answered while wiping dust off whatever outfit he saw her in. It appeared to be loose and frilly, and it covered her completely. There was neither pain nor pleasure associated with the outfit. This man's passion was a mystery to her, and that made her even more wary of him.

"Affection is unnecessary between you, but respect is mandatory." Nemesis stared sternly at the spirit. "First Female has decreed that you will learn the art of net throwing, and Antigonus is a genuine Retiarius which is, by definition, a Net Fighter. Who better to teach the skill?"

Cascadia sulked. What was so important about a net, anyway?

Nemesis wasn't done with her diatribe. "You will be his student and respect him as your Skill Master. And as for you, Antigonus, remember this spirit is not your enemy. If she fails to learn from you, you fail. You will never achieve status on the Tree of Human History. And when you return to your life, you will never find your daughter. It is the fair and just punishment."

Antigonus gasped, and Cascadia thought about the bitch word she'd heard humans use. It might apply here. But she said nothing, and the two adversaries sneered at each other as if practicing scary faces in a mirror.

"Have I made myself clear?" Nemesis sniped at them. "Answer."

"Yes, goddess," Antigonus said through tightened lips.

"Yes, goddess," Cascadia said. At least Nemesis had told her the truth: outrage was nowhere near as fun as lust.

* * *

It was mutual indignation that eventually saved them. They quietly agreed to put up with each other and get about the task at hand.

Antigonus began by demonstrating how the net worked. "It is strong hemp rope, in a circular shape. The draw string goes all around the diameter and is tied to my wrist. It allows me to pull the net tight after a throw. Or if you miss your target, you can retract the net to try again."

"You miss often, huh?" Cascadia muttered.

"No, but you will, apprentice, you will. See these lead weights tied along the diameter? They allow the net to spread open when it is thrown." He demonstrated with a clean, elegant toss that encircled a broken branch on an old log. He retrieved it then handed it to her. "Now you try."

Cascadia tossed several times and missed. She used one of the words that humans use for defecation. In frustration she took out her Bowie knife and threw it at the branch where it split the old wood straight down the middle. "Be assured, I can throw a weapon," she growled at Antigonus.

"A trident is better on the sea or open land than in the forest. It would be of little use to you so I am glad of your knife skills. I will not have to prolong our association by teaching you that, too. But you are atrocious with the net. The worst I've seen. You must concentrate and learn because it will save you where a knife will fail. Practice, apprentice, and no more backtalk."

Cascadia muttered another defecation word. She briefly wondered why humans were so fascinated with their own spoor. For the rest of the day, student and teacher walked the forest speaking only when absolutely necessary. Antigonus made her aim and chuck the net at limbs, rocks and shrubs. She continued to find him abrasive and his orders hard to stomach. Nonetheless, the next day when he made her throw the heavy net with one or both hands over a moving target, she controlled her tongue and worked hard. She'd show him, by goddess.

"The net can disable one or more enemies, silently and efficiently. If you aim well, it stops them in their tracks," Antigonus had said that morning. By afternoon, Silver Tip and the griffins grew sick of being net targets and left the area. The war games finally ended because neither warrior had the courage to aim at Nemesis.

The next morning, Antigonus moved on to another lesson. "The net has many uses." He swung it over his head and slammed it into a tree, leaving divots two inches deep in the grain of the wood. The aroma of pitch oozed from the tree wounds. "The lead weights make it nearly as powerful as a club when you swing it in a proper arc."

Cascadia's wrist was not strong enough to develop great speed or produce the depth of divots that were easy for Antigonus. After cracking the net repeatedly against tree trunks, the shock left her arm aching. A projectile of wood flew at her face and bloodied her cheek. She would have liked to quit this stupid game, to see if Aiyanna had an unguent for muscle pain, to relax in her favorite deep pool. But she would have rather died than complain or ask for mercy.

And die she nearly did when they began to fight each other that afternoon. He outmaneuvered her again and again, throwing the net easily over her while she failed to keep up with his leaps and feints. She had bruises from falls and rope burns from her embarrassing failures.

"Since you can't catch me, try to catch my trident," he commanded. "Pulling a weapon from your opponents grasp leaves him defenseless. It's nearly as good."

Cascadia heard that as a taunt, and she redoubled her efforts. But she couldn't catch him, even after he'd thrown the net and, on rare occasion, missed her. He always had time to haul it back and launch it again while she failed in her aim. She was sore, covered in sweat, nearly in tears, humiliated. Failure enraged her. Worst of all, he could tell.

"Your fury is working against you. You must control outrage, not the other way around. Stay calm, stop flailing." He drew himself up tall and swung an arm as if to a crowd. "You must have command to last in the arena or in life. Humans demand it and so do the gods."

They practiced and practiced. Finally, as the sun was about to set again, Cascadia caught Antigonus just once before he could 'kill' her. His bare foot snagged on a berry whip and he stumbled, giving her time to launch the net. It settled over his head and left shoulder as she drew it tight with all the speed and force she could muster. As he sank to his knees, her exhaustion became exhilaration. She cheered like a Coliseum crowd.

Then, with Antigonus grunting and swearing the way only warriors can do, she allowed Silver Tip to run his enormous tongue over the man's face, as though tasting him. "It's your punishment since this is just practice," she crowed. "Otherwise, he'd eat your ear. He's done that to adversaries before."

The wretched face of Antigonus nearly produced a smile amongst all the scar tissue. Cascadia thought she saw a spark of merriment in his eyes as he said, "Your skill has mastered the Master, apprentice. At least this once." When she released him, he pushed the bear away, stood, and raised his arm to her in a 'Hail, Caesar' gesture that he'd used in the Coliseum many, many times.

On their final day together, Antigonus gave her a gift. "First Female commanded that I create this for you from the gold she spun for the purpose." It was a net made of golden strands, light weight and unbreakable. It reminded Cascadia of the beautiful net on Helen of Troy's hair but, of course, much larger.

Antigonus showed Cascadia how to hurl her golden net from hiding places in the forest, around trees or from above them. It was lighter than hemp, so even the difficult pitches took less finesse. He chastised her to practice not just her aim but speed and versatility. "First Female calls this weapon the Web of Revenge, and expects you to use it against evil.

It has a magic property or two all its own, or so she told Nemesis."

Cascadia stroked the Web that she wound around her arm for safekeeping, just as she had seen him do with his own net. "It is beautiful, Antigonus. I thank you. You are a fine Skill Master." It was the first gentle statement she'd ever made to him. She was ashamed she'd been such a fractious student.

But in truth, it wasn't what she was most curious about. He had never once tried lust with her. Was she losing that skill as she gained this one? "When you look at me, what is this image you see?"

Antigonus saw the blush on her cheeks, and figured a similar shade was coloring his own. He, too, was shy about revealing the feeling she evoked in him. Finally, he answered. "When I look at you, I see a beauty, but not the kind that burns a man's loins. I am too world-weary for that." He took her hand in his and his voice trembled ever so slightly. "I see a young girl as lovely as a porcelain doll. I see my daughter."

The answer was not at all what Cascadia expected. But she had observed how animals watched over their young. "Ah. So your lust for me manifests in protection more than desire?"

Grief made the gladiator's face even more grotesque. "My daughter is another time, another place. I was enslaved and she was taken to the street brothels. I could not save her. But I must go back and continue to try. In the meantime, child, maybe I have saved you from tragedy in the days to come."

Cascadia watched the scarred and misused man turn and walk away, back into history. In his passing she understood that outrage such as his could last for centuries. Some wars would never end.

CHAPTER NINE

Shaylee Ward enjoyed the language of Blue's ears as she rode along. Ears forward was horse speak for, "I'm happy and alert." One ear back meant he was listening to her. To the side meant he was concentrating, maybe crossing a tricky bit of creek where rocks were slippery. Flat back was bad, and she'd never really seen Blue do it. It was universal horse language for, "I'm pissed and would like to kick the crap out of you." She'd seen the mares use it on him when he didn't buckle down to the harness and pull his fair share of the weight.

She rarely rode the Percheron, but today he was not pulling a ton of logs out of the woods. Their trek to her favorite hidden meadow was easy, if clambering over rocks and through streams and past patches of thorny blackberry whips could ever be considered easy. She let Blue set his own pace while she worried about the next major investment for her horse logging business. She had to face it; she needed new harnesses.

She'd put big money into the heavily padded logging collars when she'd started the business five years back. They were still good, but the harnesses were another matter. The old leather weighed maybe 70 pounds per rig and was stiff in the rain or cold. New ones cost nearly $2,000 per horse.

Shit, oh dear.

She'd heard that nylon rigs cost less, weighed less, and served the same function. She decided to assign the younger of her crew of two, Jamie Ferrell, to look into it, talk to other loggers, and find out what they thought of the newer equipment. The decision lightened her load.

The day was sunny and she was looking forward to the afternoon. When she arrived at the meadow, she slid down from Blue's back, removed her hat and wiped the dampness from her forehead. Even the Stetson couldn't repress her iron-willed curls which rebounded in the breeze that rustled through the old growth around her.

"You know where forest meadows came from?" she asked Blue as she removed his pack, unloading a tent, bedding and other camping basics. When he didn't answer she said, "They were gifts from Thunderbird. He shot lightning bolts from his eyes to open up spaces where the First People could live." She snapped a lead on the enormous horse, giving him plenty of range to nibble whatever grass he could find along the creek bank and allowing him access to water.

"No, horses didn't have a damn thing to do with it," she told him as she pitched the tent. Shaylee was at home in the forest, living and working in it most of her life. She was surrounded by native legends and logger ghost stories. And recently for Shaylee, tales of goddesses had joined her mental library. Most characters seemed more or less benign. The scariest apparition in the forest was usually the human kind.

When her campsite was set, she unpacked a rod and reel. As sunlight began to fade, she was rewarded with two rainbow trout. She put a blue enamel pan on the fire to heat water and began to clean the fish.

A tingle ran up her spine as she felt she was being watched. She looked up and around, seeing nothing. But she noticed that Blue's ears were pricked forward. *On the alert.*

A rustling in the grass was out of sync with the wind in the trees. Little forest creatures - voles and mice and ferrets - would be attracted to the trout innards. But this rustle was too loud for that. Shaylee froze in place when she heard a huff of breath, a low pitched yip. She looked up. The animal was right there. Its coat was the gray brown of a coyote, but its head was rounder and shoulders broader, more like a large dog.

Labrador, maybe. Or Rottweiler.

The coydog stared at Shaylee nervously, with eyes yellow and wise. She placed the fish guts on the ground. The half breed moved forward and bolted them down in quick gulps.

Shaylee faced the deep woods. She stood statue still, trying to see the dog's companion in the dusk. She could not say for sure at what point he materialized from the dark backdrop of the forest. She only knew he wasn't there and then he was.

He was tall and whippet lean with a loose-boned stance like a major league pitcher. His cheeks were crisscrossed with creases, skin roughened by sun and wind and life in general. Although he appeared at home in the wild, he was clean shaven with hair just

112

long enough to afford some protection from creepy crawlies.

The two people stared at each other while the coydog finished its meal. When it disappeared back into the woods, Shaylee smiled at the man and they moved into an embrace that lasted a very long time. Neither spoke but their communication was complete. Neither trusted human touch but both needed it.

Shaylee had known Blake for a long time although she was unsure whether Blake was his first or last name. He kept a small airplane at the women's compound alongside their grass air strip. In return for that, he occasionally flew one of them out when she needed a trip to civilization.

It was on the way to the compound one day that Shaylee met him in the woods. He was struggling with a wound caused when a branch snapped back at him. She'd cleaned it and given him an antibiotic cream. They'd talked like old friends. Now she brought supplies for him as well as the women.

Blake had been career military. When he returned to his home in Cascadia, town life no longer suited him. Society made little sense, didn't play by rules. He longed for structure he understood, and he found it living alone in the forest with his military-issue rifle. The rules of the wild suited Shaylee, too, although it was a lonely life for each of them. When they had met, their troubled souls reached out for solace in each other. At least for brief moments of time.

They washed off trail dust in the creek water Shaylee had heated, then Blake cooked the trout, and they shared it along with fresh picked blackberries and potatoes Shaylee had packed in on Blue. With their bellies full, the couple watched night fall. In time, the coydog reappeared and shyly moved closer to the fire. She belonged to Blake. Sort of. She rarely approached, just following wherever he went. That's why he'd named her Shadow.

"The half of her that's dog wants affection. But the wild half keeps her from accepting it," Shaylee said.

"Come, Shadow, and hear your bedtime story," Blake called to her. She stretched out her neck and allowed him to touch her ear but no more. "I tell her a tribal myth each evening, one that features a tricky coyote. I think she likes to hear them."

Shaylee laughed. "I talk to Blue, too. Maybe we're both crazy."

"All four of us. No doubt about it." Blake favored Shaylee with a slow smile, unhurried as though he were out of practice. The sadness of it melted her heart as he began his tale to the coydog.

"It's well known that Coyote is very smart. One day he saw a crow in a tree high above. It had a strip of venison. How good it would taste. So Coyote said to the crow, 'Wise one, I have been told you have a very beautiful voice. I would be honored to hear you sing to me.'

"The crow had never been called Wise One before. He gloated and preened. And he gave a little caw.

"'Oh, I am sure such a voice would thrill me so much,' Coyote said, praising the bird. 'Please sing more of a song.'

"The crow swelled up with pride. He threw back his head and burst out, 'Caw-caw! Caw-caw!' And the venison dropped from his open mouth right into Coyote's.

"Coyote swallowed it whole then said, 'You are not so wise after all. And now you will go hungry for your foolishness.' Then he trotted away, howling in laughter."

Shadow had ventured almost close enough for an ear scratch.

"Whatever made her scared of people must have been bad," Shaylee said.

Blake nodded. "Not easy for her to trust. Not easy for you or me either." Then he cleaned the plates, stretched and disappeared into the tent.

Shaylee fed Blue his grain and made sure he was securely tied for the night. Other than the *whoo-who* of a great horned owl and the breeze telling secrets in the firs, she knew they were alone. She entered the tent where Blake was already bedded down in a sleeping bag. She was so quiet, she startled him.

"Shit. You're getting as stealthy as that spirit of yours," he said. Blake was one of the very few people that Shaylee had told about Cascadia, at least as much as she remembered. She suspected First Female was messing with her memories again.

In the small amount of light from the lantern outside, Shaylee could see anticipation in his eyes. She straddled him and knelt. Her voice was a soft melody in his ear. "I think I'm seeing a new myth take shape. It's all about a handsome man that a beautiful maiden finds sleeping in the woods. He is alone, unarmed. As she begins to pull back the bedding, it releases his body heat and his scent. He smells of the woods and campfires and wildness."

"Is he afraid of her?" Blake asked in a whisper, bringing his arms up to encircle her buttocks.

Shaylee saw the litter of tattoos running down his arms to his chest, and she heard his breath quicken. But she pushed him back down. "Oh my, yes. He is so afraid he is paralyzed with it. Can't move a muscle."

"Poor him," Blake said, becoming still.

Shaylee lowered her weight onto him. "She opens his sleeping bag completely, finds him nude underneath. She runs her tongue across his chest and down his stomach." For a time, her actions spoke louder than her words.

She felt him tense and harden. After a moment, he said, "You sure he's still paralyzed?"

"She reveals her breasts, and rubs them across his lips. He is desperate to take the tender nipples into his mouth."

"Still … paralyzed?"

"Now she stands over him. He watches as she removes her jeans in a slow dance choreographed just for him. And now, her panties."

"I really think he's going to have to move pretty soon."

"At last, motion returns to his body. He lifts his arm, running his hand between her thighs. Up and up, until she can no longer stand …"

116

They continued the scene to its natural conclusion. Then they settled into the sleeping bag, arms and legs twisted around each other. Her head tucked into his neck, so close she could hardly breathe. She felt such peace, such safety.

But Shaylee knew one of them would be gone when the other awoke. Sometimes it was him, sometimes her. Neither could escape their ghosts for long, because neither could conquer the traumas from their pasts. This occasional coming together was the best they could manage. He would escape to his solitary life and she would return to her logging business.

"Do you ever want to stay?" he murmured before sleep took him down.

"Yes," she said, knowing she never would.

***

It was Blake who left the tent first, but he was not the first presence in the camp. He sucked in his breath when he saw Silver Tip with Blue. He grabbed up his rifle but noticed Cascadia sitting quietly at the campfire. He set the weapon back down.

"You know me?" Cascadia asked.

"Sort of. Shaylee told me a weird tale about a spirit and her bear. There can hardly be two of you."

"I am Cascadia."

"That's the name she used. Although her memory of her adventure with you seems to be hazy. She is still asleep." He cocked his head toward the tent.

Cascadia asked, "You two have lusted together?"

Blake snorted. "You spirits certainly are direct."

117

"Lust is … enjoyable." Cascadia smiled and gave the fire a poke with a stick as Blake made coffee. She looked down at her own body. The elixir from Helen of Troy allowed her to see herself through Blake's eyes. "In your eyes, I am in desert attire. I feel the cloth on my head. My skin is brown and damp with sweat. My muscles look very strong. This is what you lust for?"

He looked up at her in surprise. Then he turned back to the fire, watching as the water began to perk. His answer came slowly. "It was in the Middle East. She was a local, worked for us. She's dead now."

"You want to lust with me because I look like her to you?"

"No. Not really. You may look like her, but you aren't her. You're something … apart." Blake gave a quick shake of his head. "Shaylee says you're a warrior through and through. You don't need my care. Not like a human does. Not like Shaylee does."

"You prefer to lust with Shaylee than with this other woman?"

"A man can want more than one woman in his lifetime. Shaylee is this life. The freedom fighter? She was long ago."

"You have love for Shaylee?" Cascadia asked.

"Not your business, friend. Humans don't ask each other things like that. Not this human anyway."

The spirit sighed. Love was so confusing. Humans seemed to want it, but Nemesis had told her that it made them vulnerable. And Nemesis, unpleasant though she may be, only spoke the truth.

Cascadia worried for Shaylee's safety and happiness, so she tested Blake by lifting her left hand to her lips and whispering to the Ring of Gyges. She waited. Nothing happened. No glowing sapphire, no cold constricting metal. "According to the Gyges, you are not evil. I will trust you with Shaylee."

He made the bubbling sound called laughter. "Thanks. I've worried about that evil bit. Are Captain Midnight decoder rings making a comeback since I left society behind?"

Cascadia ignored his comment which she didn't understand anyway. "You can help protect Shaylee."

His laughter stopped. "What's wrong? Is she in danger?"

"All humans are."

CHAPTER TEN

The aroma of coffee awakened Shaylee. She staggered out of the tent yawning so wide she had to close her eyes. Then she rubbed away the sleep. When she opened them, she was surprised to see Blake sitting at the campfire. He looked tickled as she snapped her mouth back shut, blinked, and tried to arrange her face in a more attractive configuration.

What the ...?

This was a break in their pattern, totally against the rules. He should be long gone leaving her alone. She stretched in the chill morning air and pushed curls out of her eyes so she could squint at the clouds. Layers of gray cotton candy.

"The weather could go either way," Blake said.

Shaylee sat on an upended log next to the war vet. She grinned, feeling shy when she recalled their acrobatics the night before. "Morning."

"Cascadia and her bear were here but they wandered off a while ago." Blake handed Shaylee a cup of coffee and one of the biscuits he'd made in her old pie tin over the fire. "It's hard to buy all this spirit shit, but I guess I have to. Otherwise she's one weird chick. And I've never seen a horse and a bear gossip before."

Shaylee laughed. Blue and Silver Tip should be natural enemies, but she'd seen them stand muzzle to snout as if they were exchanging juicy secrets.

Blake poked at the fire with a stick and watched the shower of sparks. "Thought I'd walk part way back with you today."

Shaylee nodded. This was a damn strange development.

Did I forget something?

She'd brought him flashlight batteries and razors, but maybe he needed more ammunition. Or a new blanket. She couldn't imagine why else he might accompany her back toward town.

As they broke camp, the weather made its decision. A cold drizzle spit at them. Blake walked in front of the little caravan, and Shaylee followed, leading Blue. She liked hiking behind Blake, having him hold branches out of her way. If she were a Victorian lady he would no doubt bow and use his coat to ...

A bone chilling howl split the quiet.

"Shadow?" Shaylee gasped.

"Unless all that shit about werewolves in these woods is true."

Shaylee had wondered if the hairs on the back of your neck really did stand up, so she reached up and now she had her answer. Another howl chilled her bones.

Blake readied his rifle and increased his pace moving toward the sound. Shaylee jogged to keep up. Blue nickered at the increased pace and swung into an easy trot. The trail sloped upward and bent around an

121

outcropping of volcanic rock. Footing was slippery on loose stone wet from rain, and Blue's shod hooves made a loud clatter. They climbed several yards before the trail leveled off and widened.

Blake held up his hand like a soldier and halted abruptly. Shaylee, unlike a soldier, smacked into him. As she peeked around his shoulder she caught a whiff of the salty, rich odor of raw red meat.

Blood.

Shaylee saw the coydog sniffing at something on the ground. Shadow backed away, howling one last time, as Shaylee came level with Blake. Now she could see. Fur. A carcass. Death.

It was a bear, a young female not dead long enough to have been torn apart and carried away by forest creatures. A wave of sorrow swept over Shaylee. "It's a black bear ..." she began, then noticed Blake was looking at something else, his jaw clenched tight.

Something worse?

Shaylee gasped as she, too, saw the tiny carcass. "She had a cub!"

"They've both been shot," Blake said. "Not long ago. By someone who just left them behind to rot."

Stranger still, both were spread out on their backs, their legs splayed out to the sides. Shaylee looked closer. The groins of mother and baby had been shaved and sliced open. The precision of the wounds looked almost surgical.

Shaylee felt her stomach churn. She grabbed for Blake's arm. "What happened here?"

"Fucking thieves."

"What? You mean poachers did this? No way." Shaylee wasn't naive. She knew animals were poached from the forest all the time. But not like this.

Blake shook his head. "You're right. They'd take the meat. Trappers would take the fur. Trophy hunters would take the heads."

"Then what?" Shaylee heard the tension in her own voice. She wondered if it was shock making her head spin.

"I've heard of it but never seen it. This is the work of thieves stealing gall bladders."

"Gall bladder thieves? You're kidding, right?" Shaylee felt a frantic note stick in her throat. An absurd joke, surely.

"It's real all right. A member of the Nooksack tribe who lives out here once told me he's seen it."

"Poachers taking bear innards?" Maybe it was another myth like Thunderbird or the Coyote or …

"Gall bladders anyway. The Nooksack said they get around $3,000 each in Asia."

"But why?"

"Old beliefs that a bear's gall is medicine for the stomach. I guess some assholes even think it's an aphrodisiac."

Fury muscled aside confusion. "That's fucking sick. Criminal. That's like killing rhinos for their horns or elephants for their tusks." Shaylee turned her back on the horrible carnage.

"People used to eviscerate bears killed in road accidents, stuff like that. Now it's bigger business. And easy money. They kill then carry out one small body part instead of a whole bear. Harder for the law to detect. America is losing bears by the thousands."

"*Thousands?*" Shaylee's heart raced and eyes watered with outrage.

Another voice cut in. "It is my mission to find the killers. Old Man Above is furious." Cascadia materialized from the greens and browns of the forest, astride a very angry bear. Silver Tip's roar of disgust over the destruction of these two bears was far louder than Shadow's howl. The spirit hushed him, then faced Shaylee. "I greet you again, Shaylee. I require your help once more. Will you make camp again and wait here for me?"

Shaylee was briefly flustered that Cascadia wore a t-shirt emblazoned with *Show Me Your Kitties*.

"Of course I'll wait." Shaylee took her jobs seriously. Since she had been ordained as Cascadia's familiar, she could only agree even though commitments at home would soon be calling her. But Blake didn't take orders from anyone, not any more.

"It's important I do what she requests," Shaylee said to him. "But you are free to move on." She turned to the spirit. "Tell me what you need."

They went upwind from the killing ground to a spot where the path paralleled the creek again. Blake began setting up her camp while Cascadia brought Shaylee up to speed. "When Antigonus left, Nemesis gave me my mission."

"Antigonus?" Shaylee asked.

"The gladiator who was my Skill Master. He presented me this Web of Revenge." Cascadia held up her arm to display the golden net wrapped around it.

Blake gave a snort that would have made Blue proud. From the corner of her eye, Shaylee watched him drive in tent stakes. Maybe he had decided to stay. He must be worried about the bears, too.

To Cascadia, she said, "Antigonus is new to me, but I've heard of Nemesis. Something about blind justice, right?"

"Yes. Nemesis said Old Man Above has seen humans killing his bears but not for sustenance or warmth. He doesn't understand. I am to find the why and put a halt to it." She cocked her head toward Blake. "I heard what your lust partner told you about bear gall bladders. His statement has given me the why."

"Lust partner?"

"That would be me," Blake said. "Your lust partner."

"Oh," Shaylee said, still too dumbfounded about the bears to be sidetracked for long. She knew that people shot protected wildlife if a profit was to be made. They stole wild plants, too. But this was too much to believe, too low for even the nastiest weasels.

Cascadia said, "Wait for me here. I will find the killers and come back for you."

***

The Pacific Northwest area for which Cascadia was named was 750,000 square miles of land and lakes. Hikers couldn't see all its valleys and hills if they explored for months on end. Even with the magical speed and sharp vision of the rider on the flying bear, it could take many days to traverse the territory looking for an enemy.

But just miles from the first carcasses, Cascadia saw another black bear desecrated below them. And miles from that, the carcass of a grizzly.

When they landed near it, Silver Tip released an anguished cry. It was not his magnificent roar but a long, low moan. Cascadia understood he had known this bear. Whether it had been his brother or his foe, this was no way for a griz to die.

Silver Tip was devastated with grief, a wound as palpable as physical injury. Cascadia dismounted and allowed him the time he needed to mourn. He had to exorcise his anguish in his own way. The bear stampeded away.

She curled against a mossy log and trembled with emotion for him. So this was outrage. When Nemesis had explained this mission, the dark goddess had looked particularly stormy. "First Female has chosen defense of bears as the test of your outrage. It is a cruel test since you yourself depend on such an animal. Silver Tip could be a target. If you fail, he could die."

Cascadia had not fully understood until now. What if a human sliced open Silver Tip? She was even closer to him than to her two humans, Shaylee and Aiyanna. She'd been worried about them when she should have worried about *him*.

Kill her bear? The full force of outrage hit her like a blast from a volcano. First Female's goal was suddenly as clear as the blue sapphire on her finger. It was not limited to humans.

I am to be a guardian of all life in Cascadia.

What if a human slaughtered Silver Tip? What would she do to the executioner? She'd remove the man's entrails while he was alive to watch. She'd force him to eat them. She'd hack off ...

But the words of Nemesis resonated in her brain. "You must remember," the Daughter of Darkness had said. "How you handle your outrage will determine the success of your training. You cannot exact justice by committing a punishment bigger than the crime."

Cascadia ached with the need for control. Her face grew wet, and she realized her eyes were leaking in the way she'd seen human eyes do. She waited into the night for her bear to return.

Before dawn, she could wait no longer. Cold and alone, she had to go after Silver Tip. His trail was easy to follow. A grieving grizzly doesn't keep his misery to himself and she'd heard the destruction as he'd burst through all obstacles. Saplings were ripped from the ground, boulders overturned, stumps deeply gashed by powerful claws. River rocks had avalanched into a creek, creating a new dam. The path of devastation went on as long as the grizzly had the energy, and that was a very long time.

When she found him, Cascadia thought he was asleep. He was flat on his belly atop an enormous log, his legs dangling over the sides. As she approached she could see his eyes were open. Instead of shining like jet black beads, they were dull, mournful. He didn't even turn his head at her approach.

She walked up beside him and gently tugged on one of his ears. "We'll find the ones who did this, my friend." She'd heard humans use that word for others who mattered to them.

Friend.

He moaned and bumped her with his snout but other than that, he would not move. Was he just being stubborn or was something else wrong? Was he too elderly a bear to go through this misery?

Maybe he injured himself on his foray through the woods. Cascadia looked him over closely, parting the heavy fur to find a wound. She finally urged him off the log and got him to roll over on the ground onto his back. Still, she saw neither bruising nor blood.

She dropped to her knees and put her arms around his huge neck. Was he lost to her? Panic washed over her as she wrestled with a puzzle she could not solve.

"Yes, you can, little one." Cascadia heard these words as clearly as if the healer were standing beside her. "Cure this bear as I would if I were there."

"Aiyanna! Help me!"

No answer.

"I do not know what to do!"

No answer.

And then, Cascadia realized that no *sound* did not mean no answer. She already knew the answer. The healer had taught her many things. It was time she used that knowledge.

What would Aiyanna do? She'd look for a wound, of course. Cascadia had done that. What would the healer do next?

If she saw none on the outside, she'd look for a wound on the inside. Aiyana had told her that things like grief could be even harder to cure than visible injuries. That must be it! Silver Tip had a lesion to his spirit. Aiyanna would use her herb teas and secret oils for that.

Cascadia jumped up. "Rest, war bear. I will be back with a cure. I promise." She was terrified to leave him in this condition. The bear hunters could sneak right up on him. But she had medicines to make.

She gathered Solomon's seal which could help stop bleeding. Wild geranium, too, applied in a compress. Oil from many cedars was antibacterial. Or was that insect repellant? She couldn't remember for sure. As she gathered plants she watched for the human trash she sometimes encountered. Soon enough she found an empty beer can near an old campsite.

She brought everything back to Silver Tip who still lay motionless on the ground. Cascadia started a fire and boiled water in the can while she ground the plants, using a small sharp rock on a flatter one. She mixed everything, added it to the hot water, and let the concoction cool.

"Aiyanna taught me how to do this, and Aiyanna knows all things," she said to Silver Tip as she prepared the brew. He knew that Aiyanna's magic had cured his paw. Maybe he'd buy that it would cure his spirit, too, even if Cascadia had gathered all the wrong things.

I have no idea if this will work, Silver Tip. But you don't either. You just have to believe.

"Okay, open wide."

He refused.

"Just a little."

He gave the mixture a sniff.

"It smells no worse than you."

He moaned.

She ordered, "Now, war bear."

He sighed, pushing himself up into a sit. He opened his mouth and she poured in the entire contents of the can.

He swallowed. And gagged. And bellowed.

She waited two minutes recalling all the strange things she'd learned from goddesses and human warriors, things so hard to believe. But her belief in them had made them real for her. Her bear needed to do the same.

Finally, she said, "You are all better now."

Just believe.

With a shake from the tip of his blunt nose to the end of his stubby tail, he stood and snorted at her. He lowered his massive head, and rocked back and forth. His eyes began to shine with fire.

He believes!

"Your spirit is as strong as this medicine. Heartache will not topple you. We go now." Cascadia mounted the bear's broad shoulders and off they flew in an arc radiating out from the kill sites. They were back on the hunt.

* * *

The sun had climbed to mid morning when its strong cross light exposed a camp fire. Cascadia energized her invisibility. Silver Tip and she could hover above the camp but, to human eyes, would look like no more than blueness of sky and whiteness of cloud.

She saw two men below them. It wasn't hunting season, and they weren't near a trail. The site was large, looking more permanent than an overnight retreat for a couple of hikers.

Were these the bear killers?

Cascadia tried the Ring of Gyges, but the distance between the men and her hand was too great. Silver Tip was for eating them regardless, but Cascadia's ears still rang with lectures about justice. "We must know for sure," she cautioned. "We need Shaylee's help now."

Cascadia released her invisibility to conserve her energy. They flew swiftly back to the camp where she had left Shaylee. The spirit was glad to see the Blake human was still with her familiar. He had his head in her lap, and she was reading words from a book aloud to him, the way humans do. Cascadia liked his careworn face and was glad her friend had him for a lust partner. She remembered Jim Bowie. Human men had their good traits although Dogoda, spirit of the West wind was her favorite lust partner. At least so far.

When they landed, Silver Tip went off for another powwow with Blue. Cascadia explained to the humans what she had seen. Then she looked at Blake. "You have no duty to be part of this. I know you are done with war. But will you help?" She could only hope he would remember her request to protect Shaylee since she didn't want to mention it out loud. Cascadia didn't yet know a lot about humans but one thing she suspected: Shaylee would go volcanic if she knew the spirit and the man had colluded behind her back.

"I've taken too much of his time already," Shaylee said. "He doesn't stay with other ·people for long stretches of time."

Cascadia saw surprise on Shaylee's face when Blake said, "Happy to do it."

"Good. Now, can you both act?"

"Act?" asked Shaylee.

"Act?" asked Blake.

"Act," said Cascadia then explained her plan.

* * *

"You're an idiot!" the female voice whined.

"Me?" snapped the male. "Don't lay the blame on me."

"This whole stupid hike was your idea. It's getting dark, and I'm cold." Accusatory female.

"If you didn't need privacy to pee, we would never have left the trail to begin with." Exasperated male.

"Don't you dare yell at me, jerk wad." Enraged female.

"You're such a silly bitch." Enraged male.

"You're so mean to me." Sniveling female.

The arguing couple blundered into the spacious camp. Two men met them with long guns in their arms, relaxed but ready to aim if need be.

"For the love of God!" yelped the male. "Put the guns down. We mean no harm. We'll just move along."

"Oh, no! I have to pee again! We'll be going." Female in crisis mode.

"Hold it, both of you. What are you doing out here?" Gunman One glared at them but set his weapon against the base of a tree. To him, the couple must look more pathetic than threatening. But both the woman and man recognized the rifle as a .338 Winchester Magnum, more than enough to bring down a bear.

"The Missus and I are lost. She forgot to pack the trail map. If you could just give us some directions ..."

"... or let us stay here for the night since it's getting dark, and you have such a nice fire, and we have all our own food so we'd be no trouble ..."

"... then we'll be on our way at first light."

Husband and wife both looked scared of their own shadows, much less the shadows of night falling across the wilderness.

Gunman Two set down his rifle, as well. Gunman One shrugged. "I guess it'll be okay."

"As long as you stop that damn bickering," Gunman Two added.

Shaylee locked her lips with a pretend key. Her Oscar winning performance with Blake had gotten them in the door.

* * *

"I'll go," Blake whispered.

"No, me," Shaylee whispered back.

"Are we still acting?"

"No. I just think you should keep watch. You see like a damn owl at night." Shaylee threw back the sleeping bag. It must be well past midnight, and they'd heard no noises from the men's tents for a long time, other than snoring. The camp was well stocked, and she didn't want to trip over any folding stools or cooking utensils so she was very glad to have the penlight on her keychain.

While there was still some daylight, Blake had pointed out the cooler that the men had with them. It was bigger than hikers would carry although that's what these two claimed to be.

The cooler was Shaylee's target. She moved forward, circling a camp stove, extra pound-sized propane bottles, firewood, and a couple of folded tarps.

"It's right there," Blake whispered from just behind her.

"Jeeezzz," she hissed, spooky enough without him creeping up on her. "You were supposed to watch the tents."

"I am. And I'm watching you, too."

She knelt in front of the cooler and opened the two clips on the lid. She flipped it back, and they both peered inside. Then they froze. Shaylee snapped off the light just as the flap on one of the tents opened.

Gunman One, the older of the two, came out in his underwear, his pipe cleaner legs white in the weak moonlight. He wobbled off and peed mightily on a clump of blackberry bushes. With an ah and a belch and an ass scratch, he returned to his tent.

Shaylee and Blake held position for five minutes. Then, without turning the penlight on, she whispered, "Did you see inside the cooler?"

"Yes. Cheese, eggs, fish … and Ziploc bags of organs."

"Each about the size of a thumb."

"Eight of them."

They crept back to their tent. "We could leave now," Blake said. "My owl eyes can navigate."

"I don't think so. They may be threatening to wildlife, but there's no indication they're threatening to a couple of lost hikers. They don't suspect us of anything. Let's not put them on guard until we get a chance to talk to Cascadia."

Blake agreed. Then moments later he whispered, "Shaylee?"

"Mrmph?" She'd been nearly asleep.

"I think I've seen one of those guys before."

"You have? Where?"

"Don't know. But I'll think about it. 'Night."

They waited until early morning to say their good-byes to their hosts and be on their way, arguing as they left the camp just to keep up appearances. Neither had slept much. But Shaylee had enjoyed the role playing with Blake and lying there next to him doing nothing more strenuous than holding on to him.

But that was the trouble, wasn't it? Just holding on was more of a strain than she'd ever been able to handle. And this one night was not going to change that.

CHAPTER ELEVEN

Blake was gone by midday when Cascadia reappeared. Shaylee was packing up, ready to move on with Blue. She had a logging job that started the next day, and she had to get back to River Junction to call her crew with directions to the new site. It was a tricky job, removing diseased trees from the midst of healthy growth in a swampy low spot. It was too precise a process for traditional logging companies, but perfect for a horse crew who could serpentine its way between the trees.

"Where is your lust partner?" Cascadia asked.

"Back in the forest." Shaylee knew he had to go. Of course he did. He'd been with her longer than usual. He had to go. Of course he did.

But still.

She told Cascadia that they'd found the gall bladders of bears at the camp the spirit had seen from the air. That there were two gunmen. That their guilt in the illegal trafficking was in little doubt.

"Then I will find them again. I request another favor. I must leave Silver Tip with you for a time."

"Leave him? I must not have heard you right."

"I fear for him. He is in danger from these men. More than I am. They do not seem to seek spirit gall bladders."

Shaylee looked at the half ton of ursine muscle and said, "You know, Cascadia, that's not like asking someone to take care of your chihuahua. Besides, he won't stay here under my orders. I can't even keep a goddamn *man* here."

"He will stay under mine."

But that didn't mean he'd like it. As Cascadia said whatever the hell she said to him, the grizzly reared to his full height and roared a mighty roar, bear spittle flying like fetid rain drops. He swiped the air just over Cascadia's head, claws coming so close they ruffled her hair. He bared his teeth revealing incisors that could easily pierce to the bone, took her arm in his mouth and shook it gently. He released her but backed far away then sprinted toward her at a startling speed. Cascadia simply stood her ground until he veered away.

Finally his tantrum abated. His posturing was done. When Cascadia said his name, he came to her, head down like a supplicant dog.

Blue whinnied and the bear slunk away to his buddy for comfort. Shaylee figured they were having a discussion about which was harder to understand – a human or a spirit.

* * *

Cascadia tracked the men on foot, along a narrow game trail. A bear print was identifiable by the five claw marks on each paw. She knew bears were smart and wary, based on her experience with Silver Tip. They could smell, hear and see just fine. But most of them couldn't fly.

The spirit caught up with the hunters when they stopped at a hillside meadow, a natural break in the trees where the rocky ground only supported shrubs, grasses and wildflowers. They unloaded their gear and tucked themselves beside a fallen log not far from a large patch of ripe huckleberries. The younger man was using a hunter's distressed rabbit call. This was bear heaven. An easy morsel of meat followed by a sweet huckleberry dessert.

The two sat back-to-back watching opposite directions for a bear's approach. Cascadia heard the older one say to the younger, "Keep an eye out for cougars. Big cats like wounded bunnies, too." Young One had thick black curls and a sweet round face. He looked more like a farm boy than a vicious killer. The other, middle-aged and showing it around the belt, could have been his father or an uncle scuffed up by passing time.

Cascadia observed them from the cover of cedar boughs. She was in no hurry, waiting to spring her trap in a way that would make Antigonus proud. To assure herself of their guilt, she put the Ring of Gyges against her lips and whispered the secret words. The two bands of metal and sapphire became icy, so cold that they contracted on her finger to the point of pain. The sapphire glowed a brilliant blue. Now she had no doubts at all that these were the bear killers.

It was time to make her move. She energized her invisibility and moved away from the tree to stand firmly on the trail before them. Antigonus had lectured repeatedly about a balanced stance to throw the Web of Revenge. She began to unwrap the golden weapon from her arm, but then she froze.

A black bear ambled into sight, crossing the meadow between the men's location and her own. He was small but fattening himself for the coming winter. The berry patch would do just fine. He was alert, but he could not scent the men who were downwind.

Making no fast moves, the hunters slowly raised their guns. But the bear abruptly reared up, spun around and focused toward the old cedar tree. Cascadia was upwind, so the bear easily pinpointed her by scent if not by sight.

Busted.

The men stared in her direction, looking for whatever distracted the bear. Old One started to stand. A successful swing of the Web was blocked by the bear so Cascadia pulled her Bowie knife from the white sheath on her belt and launched it. She aimed the flying death to stop them, not to kill them. It sliced through the collar of the younger man, pinning him to the fallen log behind him. His shocked yelp alerted the bear. It swiveled toward the men, rose to its hind feet and assessed the situation. Charge them or run? Fight or flight?

Cascadia shrieked, "get out" at the bear as she ran past it and the Web of Revenge over her head to release it. It flashed golden light in the sun as it flew, startling men and bear. The Web dropped over Old One's head and expanded down to Young One who was pinned to the log. Cascadia gave a mighty pull then tied the drawstring to the trunk of the cedar.

The bear spun forward then back. Not understanding the situation, it would attack whatever scared it most ... the danger it could smell or the one it could see. Meanwhile, Young One dropped his rifle and began digging at the net. Panic must have kept him from concentrating on the knife. Cascadia held out her hand. The blade wrenched itself free and returned to her.

"What the fuck! Who threw this net? And that knife ... it flew backwards!" Old Man struggled to free his gun from entanglement and fired a wild shot before he, too, dropped his weapon to grab the Web. The loud bang in the quiet meadow terrified the young bear who galloped away at the speed of a horse. The huckleberries just weren't worth this craziness.

Cascadia grabbed both guns and threw them out of reach. As the men clutched at the net to remove it, she warned them – Nemesis would have said it was the fair thing to do. "Do not fight the Web, humans."

They continued to tug and twist, so the Web of Revenge revealed the magic properties granted it by First Female. It stuck to their hands like a spider web to a fly. For good measure, it stung. The more entangled they became, the more pain they brought on themselves. Their cries ricocheted through the meadow. Old One used words that were new to Cascadia, words about anuses and fornication and mothers. Maybe Blake could explain this man talk to her later.

They cut at the net with their own hunting knives, but it swiftly encased the weapons in a gooey cocoon of golden floss. Both tried to pick the net off their arms only to find their fingers stung with each attempt.

Finally, Cascadia spoke. "Be still, and it won't hurt you. Get on your knees, humans."

"Do as she says, Dad," said Young One between sobs.

"She who, for fuck sake? Who's there?" Old One roared, armed with more fight or less sense than his son.

"She's right. It doesn't hurt if you stay still." Young One pulled his father down and hung on to him until he, too, settled. They struggled to see their captor, peering through the golden strands of the net with eyes so wide the whites showed all around.

Young One gasped, "It's a *ghost*."

"No. A girl. Just a girl. Come out, sister."

" I can't see her ..."

"But she's there. Somewhere."

Cascadia spoke. "You have broken the code of Old Man Above and First Female."

"The code of who the hell? Why can't we see you?"

"What's she talking about, Dad?"

"What you talking about, girlie? Come on out."

Cascadia heard more anger than fear in the father's voice. She answered, "You have murdered bears for nothing but your own greed."

"Judas priest. You can't murder bears. They're just animals."

Outrage flooded her like a torrent of lava as she thought about what had happened and what could happen to Silver Tip if these two were allowed to continue. "I am deciding whether to kill you." She wanted to. She couldn't imagine how these humans could serve any good purpose. But Nemesis lectured in her brain: do not allow justice to become injustice.

"You can't kill us for killing bears, girlie. And who says that's what we're doing? Guns are for our own protection."

"Yeah, yeah, that's it. Self-protection," chimed in Young One. A stain of urine spread across his pants.

The most terrible roar rattled the trees and the hills. Cascadia was surprised. She said to the men, "A greater fear than a bodiless voice and a stinging net is on its way."

Silver Tip landed with a bear sized thump next to the invisible spirit. She turned to him and snapped, "I told you ..."

"Grrr-rowl, snert," he cut in.

"Well, if First Female said ..."

"Rrrrahrrr."

"Yes, she's my boss, too, but ... "

"Aaauuuwww."

"Okay, okay. I won't leave you again."

"Jesus, Dad," cried Young One. "We've been taken by aliens."

Cascadia said, "This bear would like to kill you by eating you alive, beginning with your gall bladders. I could let him. But I have another idea."

She remembered the evil man who had a spider tattoo on his neck, the one she had met not so long ago. Tattoos. Yes, that would do. It would not kill the men, but it would serve to keep them away from any more bears. And that was the point, wasn't it? To stop the slaughter?

"Instead of killing you, I think I will permanently scar you. A tattoo of sorts, one that any spirit or god in the woods will recognize. If one of them sees you here again, you will die."

"Tattoos? What kind of tattoos?" The terror on their faces seemed to say a stinging net was preferable to mutilation.

"This bear would like them placed on your testicles. But I will use your foreheads, easy for all to see." She drew her Bowie knife and held it up to be sure they both saw the wicked sharp blade. Three slashes on each man ought to do nicely.

But Silver Tip huffed again.

She turned toward him.

He whined.

"Oh, all right. You do it."

The grizzly approached the men. They shrunk back, but the web stung them again until they stayed still. They cried. They begged for mercy.

Only two of Silver Tip's long arched claws contacted their skin. His paw was too big for all five to fit unless he peeled back their faces completely. And he knew he was not to kill them. Instead, he raked each across the forehead, leaving deep gashes. Silver Tip did the younger first, snarling as the man howled in pain. When it was his turn, the older one tried to muffle his own cries, but he failed. The deep welts would mark father and son for life.

It was not yet over. Screeching and a whirlwind from beating wings emanated from above. The griffins halted and the tall goddess in the dark veil looked down on the scene; next to her stood Antigonus. The old gladiator cheered Cascadia as if she were a warrior in the Coliseum. Nemesis ordered her to look for the men's cooler. She found it amid their gear, removed the bags of bear bladders, then lifted them up to Nemesis.

The Goddess spoke. "Old Man Above ordered me to take these bear remains to Ursa Minor, where they will join the she-bear in protection of the Pole Star. It will shine a little brighter now. He honors his fallen creatures and thanks you, Cascadia, for stopping these humans. And I assess the punishment you have bestowed to be just. Well done, Spirit." The chariot disappeared into the clouds.

The humans were too dumbfounded to question what had just happened and in too much pain to care. Cascadia removed the ammunition from their guns and the Web of Revenge from the disfigured men. She dropped their packs in front of them while Silver Tip maintained his watch on father and son.

Over their moans she said, "Go now. The nearest village is six miles to the northwest. If you hurry, you may get to antibiotics in time. Bandage yourselves as best you can so you won't bleed out. Once you are gone, never come into these woods again. The gods will be watching."

They rose and staggered off, trying to keep blood out of their eyes. Cascadia watched until they disappeared, then listened for any indication they were coming back. Meanwhile, she gave one of their guns to Silver Tip. Like a huge pup with a plush toy, he happily chewed up its synthetic stock and grip, and bashed it repeatedly against rocks. It would never shoot straight again.

The men hadn't killed humans, so she hadn't killed them. But she stopped their slaughter of bears. Shaylee, who bristled at the idea of killing a human, would approve.

Cascadia considered what she had learned about human emotion. Lust was a good thing until it was taken too far. Outrage was a good thing until it was taken too far. Pushed to the extreme, good became bad. Was this the key to human behavior? Were they being pushed too far?

Cascadia sighed. She'd understand more as other teachers taught her other things. In the meantime, she had let the hunters go. Maybe they would die of their wounds before they made it back to their village. Maybe not. It was no longer her concern.

When Silver Tip was done with his chew toy, she took the other rifle, climbed on his back, and they flew away.

* * *

Blake watched the whole thing from the trees. He was downwind so Silver Tip did not smell him, and Cascadia did not see or hear him. He was impressed by her performance with the Web of Revenge. "You're one tough warrior, kiddo," he whispered.

Now he had work to do. Blake was a retired soldier, never counseled by a goddess with justice in mind. Instead, he'd been conditioned to destroy any adversary.

Cascadia was naïve about humans. Blake knew these two men would come back to hunt again once their fear had faded. This time, their target would include revenge against Silver Tip. Cascadia, too, if spirits could be murdered. He couldn't let that happen. He didn't understand how, but the welfare of the spirit was somehow important to the welfare of Shaylee. He didn't need to understand in order to protect.

Blake and Shadow followed the trail of father and son. Even if he lost them for now, he'd finally remembered where he had seen the older man before. He was the veterinarian from a nearby village. No wonder the incisions on the bear carcasses had looked so precise.

Blake smiled. It felt good to be hunting again.

* * *

By early evening, Cascadia arrived at Aiyanna's cabin. The stoop-shouldered healer was stirring an odiferous pot on her wood stove and muttering to a recipe book, its pages yellowed with use and time. "Now where did I put that burdock root?"

"On the highest shelf," Cascadia said.

Aiyana looked up startled, then joy lit her face. "So you are back." Her smile soon faded as she peered at the spirit. "They've taught you lessons hard to learn. I see it in your face. A scar to your cheek. Sadness in your eyes. And maybe fear."

I must no longer be quite so plain. Battle scars.

"Yes. Nemesis has taught me outrage."

Aiyana sighed. "I might could cure that. But I best not. If they feel you need it."

"It is outrage that has brought me here." Cascadia had worried about Aiyana since her lessons with Nemesis. She could not rid herself of the image Nemesis had projected into the meadow pool, the vision of a mob burning Aiyanna as a witch.

She knew the healer had been a dedicated nurse, one finally sickened by hospital politics and paperwork, drug companies and chemicals. Aiyanna had bucked the system until the system booted her out. She'd retired to this cabin, alone and disillusioned. Yet, she still helped troubled humans who found their way to her door for herbal ointments and fragrant oils to cure what ailed them. Neither the medical community nor religious institutions thought she had any right to be doing this.

Was the image a premonition or merely a warning created by Nemesis as part of her lesson plan? Cascadia didn't know, but she took no chances.

"I want you to keep this rifle," she said to Aiyanna, holding out the weapon she had taken from the hunters, the one Silver Tip had not destroyed.

"But why? I already have Old Guts 'n Glory," Aiyanna said pointing at the shotgun in the rack hanging on the cabin wall. Cascadia had made its acquaintance when she first met the healer.

"Nemesis showed me a vision. I think she was just teaching me a lesson, but … I want you safe."

Aiyanna took the rifle and leaned it against the wall behind her door. "I'd never shoot someone, Cascadia. Not really. I've spent too many years patching people up to start blowing them apart."

"The gun is not for you. It is for me. You must teach me how to use it. Just in case. I will keep it here."

Aiyanna put her arms around the slender body. "I don't know whether you can feel my hug, Cascadia. Maybe a spirit's substance has no sense of touch. But I do know that you are learning to care about people as much as I do. Let's hope neither of us has to kill."

Cascadia enjoyed the hug but did not tell Aiyanna that she already had killed a man named Spider.

* * *

Shaylee was holding the long reins, trotting behind Blue and Violet as they hauled two massive logs over a deadfall. "Come on, you two," she called to them. "Oats at the end of the trail."

Blue swung one ear back, listening to her. Then he turned his head, pointed his ears on alert and stared at a spot next to her. With no other warning, Cascadia was there.

"Crap! You have to stop doing that," Shaylee gasped, nearly stumbling over the logs.

"I make you nervous?"

"Appearing out of thin air? In a *Motel Hell* t-shirt? Why would that make me nervous?'

"What I have to say may test your nerve even more. I'm here to warn you." Cascadia told her about the image from Nemesis of an abusive uncle coming to hunt her familiar down.

Shaylee went pale. "How has he found me? When will he come?"

Cascadia shrugged. "I think he may not appear at all, that the story was meant more as a lesson than as foreseeing the future."

Shaylee relaxed. A little. Knowing he might one day return was a horror story she lived with.

Cascadia continued. "If he ever does come back, he has more than a little girl to confront. He faces two fine gladiators. He faces you and me. Together."

* * *

"No. I think the green next to the yellow. Before the blue." First Female stood back to squint at the rainbow Old Man Above was helping her create. She'd finally talked him into painting. One end of the brilliant arc dipped into her new Storm King Mountain lake. The other disappeared over the mountain to the sea. "And then the indigo just over the violet."

"Make up your mind," he muttered, moving the swash of yellow one arc higher and the indigo two lower. Full voice he added, "Yes, my divine one. That's better. I think you are right."

"Speaking of right, Nemesis was here with a request," First Female said.

Old Man Above grunted at the name. He didn't always act fairly and felt the daughter of darkness disapproved of him. "She's quite sour, don't you think? So picky, picky."

"Her disapproval is, in fact, why she came," First Female said while holding the orange and red up to the sunlight and cocking her head in deep consideration. "She requests that we change history on behalf of Antigonus."

"The gladiator? A slave? Isn't that a lowly use of my considerable talent? *Our* talent?" Old Man Above took the orange and unfurled it across the yellow.

"She considers him a good man who has been dealt with too severely. History has him dying in the arena, old and broken. Worse yet, he is mortified as the target that trainees practice on. Nemesis requests that, instead, he be allowed to fight on until he is so revered that the emperor frees him. And that his daughter be allowed to find him and care for him the rest of his days."

"Hmmm," said Old Man Above. "Well, Nemesis is the expert in fairness. I suppose we could go a little easier on the man. And if his daughter is allowed to live, her descendants may do a better job than the ones they'll replace."

The two stood back, looking at their work so far. "Just one last thing, I think, to make it rival even the Northern Lights in glory." Together they rolled out the red to cap the rainbow, all shiny with rain and sun. Then they sat in the foothills just watching the thunderheads circle, admiring this newest creation. "Perfection," First Female declared.

"Speaking of fairness. Your spirit did well to punish the assassins of my bears, even though the human male delivered the final blows." Old Man Above thought about crime and punishment but it was too abstract for him so he stopped trying. He just knew he was happy his bears were safe.

"Cascadia thinks some humans lack the ability to control emotion. And uncontrolled emotion inhibits their ability to empathize, to feel compassion."

This abstraction was well beyond Old Man Above.

First Female sighed a wind that tugged the last of the autumn leaves off the deciduous trees and cartwheeled them across the land. "This issue with empathy may be the mistake we made in their creation. Maybe they can be taught it. Or maybe we will need to obliterate them all and reformulate the ooze we use for their brains." First Female took one last look then rolled up the rainbow until she next wanted to view it. "Cascadia may one day have to deal with Blake's ease in taking lives. As will Shaylee. If that day arrives, spirit and familiar could become enemies instead of friends."

"Ah," Old Man Above said with approval. "Now that adds a dash of color to the story! I can't wait to see what happens next."

PART THREE

Wherein the Horde of Goodness
fights for dominion
and the thing with feathers is sorely tested

CHAPTER TWELVE

Old Man Above was tossing rings around Saturn while his lava loaf bubbled and spit. Between throws he said, "Dinner will be ready soon, my heart's delight."

"You know I don't eat junk food," First Female replied. "Besides, I'm far too upset." Her tears rained down, creating a torrential flood on the land below.

Old Man Above was suddenly aware he was unaware of what troubled her now. Something he'd done or not done? Said or not said? Best to grovel just in case. "I am so, so sorry. My memory is not what it once was. I am a lowly toad, a scum-covered pestilence, a – "

"Oh, shut it. For once, the problem isn't you." She dried her eyes on the nearest cloud.

"Then how can I help? What can I do? I'm at your command. I aim to please." He hoped this was sufficient sniveling to cover his infractions for many moons to come.

"The time is near for our spirit Cascadia to tell us what is wrong with our humans. They seem more out of control than ever. They steal, they lie, they abuse, they murder, they despise each other's beliefs. Even here in Cascadia, matters have gotten worse. One nest of them is actually enslaving others." She sighed a chill wind that dropped early snow along the spine of the mountains. "How can one little spirit handle all of it? Maybe this quest has failed. I'm afraid it is all quite hopeless."

Old Man Above had never before heard First Female sound so bereft. "Both you and the humans need a refill of hope. I shall locate it for you. Elpis is her name, right? The Goddess of Hope?"

"I would, of course, consult Elpis, but I can't find the silly little shapeshifter."

"Has Pandora got her in that damn box again?"

"It's the first place I looked. But Elpis isn't there. Ever since that unpleasantness, she hides herself away in any nook or cranny she can find."

"I'll locate her, my precious." Old Man Above called up two of his favorite war dogs to lead the hunt. First and most fierce came the Hound of Hades, the three-headed Cerberus. One snout growled, another scented the wind, and the third howled like a banshee as the hound bounded away on the trail of Hope. But it was King Arthur's old boar hunter Cavall, calmer and wiser than the excitable Hell Hound, who first snuffled his way to the Tree of Human History. He presented himself at the desk of Emily Dickinson long before Cerberus thrashed into the room, furiously wagging its dragon-like tail.

"Shut your yaps, mongrels," the poet snapped. "Can't you see I'm rhyming? Don't you hear that fly buzz? "

"Boooooowwwww," howled Cerberus head number one.

"Yip, yappity yip," snapped head number two, representing a far more excitable breed.

154

Head number three was momentarily busy scratching an ear with a hind paw.

Cavall, good boy that he was, executed a play bow impossible to ignore. He wagged his tail and lolled his tongue and cracked a toothy smile. It worked every time; humans were so easily charmed.

"Oh all right," Emily sighed. She looked up, pointed and said, "Hope is the thing with feathers."

There, from a swing within an ornamental birdcage, Elpis peeked out through the bars. A garland of tiny blossoms ringed her fluffy locks and her fairy-sized wings trembled, the downy feathers fluttering with nerves or air currents. Neither Emily nor Cavall could tell which. Her cheeks were chubby and lineless as a cherub's, quite unusual in a goddess.

Miss Dickinson lifted the cage and handed it to Cavall. "Depart before I slide the bolt upon the door."

The great canine took the golden enclosure by its hanger, then sped across time and space to deliver Elpis to Old Man Above. Elpis whoopty-dooed throughout the ride, whether from fear or joy Cavall never knew. Cerberus followed far behind, heads snapping at each other, empty pawed.

Old Man Above took the cage from Cavall and sent the trusted canine back to King Arthur's side. "Beware the great boar's tusk when you corner him, my friend," he warned. Then he rushed through the glistening Passage of Rainbows, looking for First Female.

"Good news, my endless love," he called, beaming with pride. "Hope has arrived."

* * *

Cascadia was slumbering atop Silver Tip whose great grizzly girth was a soft furry bed. She had become used to his beary odor. Turning on her side and smacking her lips, she suddenly knew she was no longer alone on the bear. Her eyes snapped open.

The wisp of a creature was right there at the end of her nose, waving chubby little arms for attention. "Yo! Good morning and hello!" the being nattered in a voice as lyrical as a Pied Piper tune. "I'm Elpis. Howdy do to you!"

Cascadia sat up and looked again. Was this chattering creature some kind of squirrel? One with the courage to draw near to a bear? The size was right but yellow feathers seemed wrong. Then the spirit noticed the being's wings and guessed, "You are a flying squirrel!"

"Nix and no, nor bat nor bird I be, no siree." The creature lifted off the ground and spread her wings which grew to the four foot span of a great horned owl. She flapped slowly in a circle around the shady pool in the meadow, but as she soared her size shrank to that of a pudgy bug. "Nor do I be a bumblebee."

She lit on top of a golden bird cage, which had magically appeared on the ground cover next to a sleeping Silver Tip. "May I come aboard? My stars, you're easier on the feet than these bars."

Cascadia nodded and Elpis winged her way into the spirit's hand, settling there to the size and shape of a Granny Smith apple. Cascadia lifted her palm to her eyes to peer closely at this captivating shapeshifter.

"Phew! Do you know how hard it is for a feathered fat fairy to fly like that? One must be an acrobat," Elpis said, wiping her brow in emotive exaggeration. "Thanks for the gift of a lift. Now, as I was saying, I'm Elpis, Goddess of Hope."

"I am Cascadia."

The tiny goddess squinted up at the spirit's face. "Good golly, you're plain. No offense ... I understand the whys for your countenance. I'm no Helen of Troy myself. But I'm as pleased as she to be the next to teach and preach."

The voice of Elpis was so irritatingly cheery that Cascadia worried Silver Tip might awaken to squash her with a grumpy paw. She had heard humans talk about morning people. "You seem very happy this morning."

"Sis, I feel bliss most of the time. Can't stay sad for long. A frown's down but giddy's up, that's what I always say." Her grin exposed teeth as perfect as seed pearls.

"You look young," Cascadia said, eyeing the smooth, clear skin of the goddess.

"Yes, good skin, I guess. Hope keeps me young, plus sweet songs I have sung and staying out of direct sun and a rub of mountain mint with a hint of adder's tongue and vomit of bees which humans please to call honey. Isn't that funny? Anyway, truth be told, I'm thousands of years old."

All this swooping of wings and chipper prattle finally disturbed Silver Tip. He yawned and lifted his great self, dumping Cascadia to her feet. The bear scratched his chest with claws that could kill, squinted at Elpis, but saw no reason to slay her at the moment. She was less than a bear-sized bite, and all those feathers did not look tasty. So he ambled off to do what bears do in the woods, then to seek out a breakfast of juicy grubs and salmon berries.

Cascadia turned her attention back to the shapeshifter and to a word she had never heard before. "You called yourself a feathered fat fairy. What is the meaning of this word you used, this *fat*?"

"Chubby, tubby, junk in the trunk. Like brother bear, there," Elpis pointed toward the ample rump of the departing Silver Tip. Then she danced, switching her hips to the beatbox rhythm of her lips and tongue. Her feathery yellow robe swirled and danced while a puff of glittery dust floated all about her.

"Oooff," she said at the end of her dance, collapsing back into Cascadia's palm. "It's your duty to have a good sized booty if you want to dance like that. But it's not at all about what I eat, my sweet." Elpis patted her downy self back into place and the fairy dust settled down. "We fairies don't ingest. I'm portly by birth, but I digress."

Cascadia thought Elpis was funny and she laughed the gurgling sound she had learned from humans. Was that why she liked the fairy goddess or was it the other sensation she felt? The one that caressed her with contentment? Made her feel like purring. What was that about? Whatever it was, Elpis enchanted Cascadia with her chatter. "People and spirits and gods. I am why you strive to beat odds, refuse to give in until you win, keep failure on a very short rope. I am Hope."

Elpis radiated a bonhomie that made Cascadia feel capable and joyful. Maybe it was caused by that hint of glittering dust in the air.

"You are here to teach me about hope?" Cascadia was delighted at this turn of events, considering what a downer Nemesis had been.

"Yes, indeedy, sweetie. So let's begin the tale to spin." Elpis scrambled onto a boulder that Helen of Troy had used before to lecture the spirit when just a newbie. As Hope climbed up and sat, she became the size of a garden gnome. Meanwhile, Cascadia settled into the groundcover at her feet.

Elpis told the story of Pandora, the first human female who opened a famous container and spilled all the world's ills onto humanity. "But I stuck like a burr, yes sir, to the inside of the jar. Pandora could neither shake me loose nor cast me afar." Elpis was the reason that humans through the worst of times, be it malady or mayhem, famine or failure, disgrace or disease, still had hope to guide them. "Like an ancient Greek said with me in mind, '"Hope is the only good god remaining among mankind.'"

"Because of you, humans have hope today."

"Well, it's always been so but now, oh woe, I don't know. A battle brews that your humans may lose. That's where you and I come in. We must replenish human hope if their goodness is to win." At this Elpis pulled a milkweed pod from her pocket and split it open. Downy parachute seeds dispersed in the air. But no, not seeds. Droplets of golden powder rained on Cascadia who sighed with wellbeing. She felt an internal warmth like the one created by the elixir from

Helen of Troy. But this tenderness affected her mind not her body.

Elpis somersaulted off the boulder, now small as a marmot. Cascadia was bewitched by the change in size. "Hope is sometimes big and sometimes small?"

"Hope comes in the size to suit, from a thimble to a skinful."

Cascadia felt confused. She'd thought she was getting a handle on emotion. "The Goddess of Lust and the Goddess of Justice have both taught me how feelings work. That a human with too much emotion like lust or judgment lacks empathy for anyone else."

"About hope, they're wrong as rain, and I'll explain. For better or worse, hope works in reverse. The more the merrier. Humans are running low and nothing's scarier. We need to help them get it back, that's a fact."

"We can do this? Bring hope back?"

"We can try. Can't say I'm eager to see hope die."

CHAPTER THIRTEEN

Shaylee Ward heard the man tearing through the underbrush before she saw him. He was obviously angry, and if he was a stalker, he was a crazy one. Most gave up long before they got this close to the woman's compound hidden so deep in the woods. The women called it Bird Woman because the one who ran it helped them fly away. Also, Shaylee assumed, because the leader's name was Wren Grisholm.

Shaylee didn't know this man's story, didn't want to. She was sorry to see him way out here in the forest where she and Blue brought supplies and offered assistance. Wren had asked her to help stop this guy before she returned home. And Shaylee could not refuse. So here she was, squatting in damp moss behind a fallen nurse log.

The man passed Shaylee. Then Wren stepped out of the forest directly in front of him.

"What the fuck!" he said, drawing up short in surprise.

Wren held up her hand, and said, "Please stop. This is private property. You're not wanted here."

"You scared the shit out of me, old woman," he said, recovering his composure. "I'm looking for my wife. Allison Shelton."

"No one else is here. Now turn back. You're trespassing."

"ALLISON, YOU FUCKING BITCH!" the man shrieked at the top of his lungs. "GET YOUR ASS OUT HERE."

"Enough! Turn back. I won't ask again."

He looked at her with disdain, saying, "No problem handling old meat like you." Without warning, he lunged.

The stun gun that touched the back of his neck delivered a punch of nearly a million volts. He collapsed instantly, falling on top of Wren, his large bulk blanketing her small one.

"Get Bluto off me," Wren snapped, wrestling with the limp body.

Shaylee put the stun gun in her pack then helped roll the man onto the ground. As Wren stood and brushed herself off, Shaylee stared at the stalker's face. He looked glassy eyed as a fish on a hook, his lips moving slightly. She said, "We have less than ten minutes."

The two women began to undress the stalker, aware he could hear but do nothing about it until his body recovered from the shock they had delivered. Each of them undid a boot, then pulled off a pant leg. When they were done, the stalker was down to boxers. His knife and a 9mm Beretta lay on the pile of his clothes. "Good gun. Glad to have it for the camp," Wren said, picking it up to examine.

Shaylee secured his hands behind his back with plastic zip ties. As he began to recover control of his motor functions, Wren said, "Okay, asswipe. You

162

didn't listen the first two times you were told to turn back. This is the last time. Sit up." She grabbed his hair, helping pull him into a sitting position. Then she held his gun to the back of his head. "You're aimed in the right direction. Go that way, and you'll find your way out."

"Sh-Shit. You can't leave me like this," he moaned, shaking his head as though trying to clear it.

"Oh, but we can. Don't panic and you'll figure a way to remove the cuffs. If you're lucky or just want to survive bad enough, you won't die from insect bites or infection from nettles or any other kind of exposure. If you're not so lucky, you'll wander for days. Starvation, polluted water, bears, cougars. Lots of ways to die."

He began to whine. "But how can I get back? What will – "

"I just don't care about that. But I do know, if you come this way again, you'll die for sure. Now remember, you're aimed in the right direction. Don't screw it up."

Wren and Shaylee picked up his boots, knife and clothes. Wren put the handgun in her backpack and they walked away. They were accompanied by the man's angry cries until he was beyond ear shot.

"No wonder his wife is a runaway," Wren said. "Who wouldn't want to leave him?"

"Yeah. Even old meat like you."

"Fuck you, too."

The women's laughter relieved their stress.

"I'll let Blake know he's on his way. He'll help him out if he hasn't lost the cuffs by tomorrow."

"Before you go, I need to tell you about a girl we lost," Wren said. "It's bad."

A lot that Wren had to say was bad. But this time, Shaylee was horrified.

* * *

Shaylee retrieved Blue and her wagon from the Bird Woman compound then headed back through the forest toward her home. It was late afternoon, but the muscular young horse could make it before nightfall. The wagon was lightweight, empty on this flip trip. "You know the way to carry the sleigh," Shaylee sang off key to the Percheron while she sat in the wagon on a wooden box that doubled as an inflexible bench seat.

Shaylee became involved with Bird Woman because she believed no female in the land of the free should live in fear of a man, although she herself had done just that for a long time. As she grew to adulthood, she thought Uncle Carson would find her, that she'd awaken in her bed with him on top of her. Nightmares had been her constant reality. Sometimes still were.

Time had helped. Time and counseling and confidence in her own abilities to be a strong, independent woman. But emotional damage had been done. Shaylee might still trance out if overstressed, and she trusted few males.

"Yes, I trust you, Blue," she said to the horse. He turned an ear to listen to her. "And my crew. And Blake, I think. I trust him. Maybe."

Putting herself in danger from the Bird Woman husbands, standing firm against them, helped her deal with her own dreads. Uncle Carson couldn't scare her into submission anymore. "At least I don't think he could. Bastard would probably have no interest in a grown-up female anyway."

The big horse snorted, blowing air through his lips.

"What? No, I am not old. Thirty is old for a horse but it's prime time for a human."

The story Wren had told her of a woman stolen from Bird Woman had probably brought on these thoughts about her uncle, her cousin, and how people in general couldn't be trusted with each other. Maybe she could talk about it with Cascadia one day, the way you'd share a problem with a human friend. "Not that you aren't a friend, Blue. But this is girl stuff I'm talking about."

By the time they got back to the barn, Shaylee was glad to be tired. She settled Blue down then headed to the house where she planned a long night's rest before a hard day of logging. "I gotta get a cushion for that damn box," she muttered, rubbing her backside as she climbed the stairs to her bedroom.

* * *

The next morning, Shaylee was in a gloomy mood. A good night's sleep had not been in the cards. First Female had intruded in a dream or in a vision or in a trance. Shaylee was never sure how the Presence revealed herself because her brain often felt cloudy following their encounters. As if First Female erased keywords.

But last night's message cut through the fog like a laser: a war in the woods was coming. A force of

165

good against a force of evil. The rules of engagement would not be pretty.

"This conflict, like most, will have gray areas which should never be dug at too deeply," First Female had said or projected or communicated in a voice sadder than a dirge. "Gray areas much like the murder of Spider and the outcome for the men who sought gall bladders of bears."

She made it clear that Shaylee would fight alongside Cascadia in this conflict. Then, win or lose, the spirit would decide the fate of mankind. "If she finds no way to cure your species of the evil in your souls, Old Man Above and I may bring you all to a volcanic end."

The sad music died and the Presence was gone. But Shaylee understood full well.

Well that shits bricks. I'm to honcho a battle that will set humans straight or our geese are all cooked in a cauldron. No pressure there.

The gloomy mood followed her through morning chores. She thought about death in the forest as she checked Blue's new nylon harness for any sign of fraying where straps passed through rings. "Always have been countless ways to die around here," she muttered.

"What did you say?" Jamie Farrell asked while he worked a snaffle bit between Violet's big lips. The roan snorted then nipped at him. He dodged then patted her muzzle.

"Oh, nothing important." But it *was* important. From the very beginning of human history, native tribes had suffered starvation or murder at the hands of intruders, including each other. The old growth forest, cloaked in fog and chilling mist, next took the lives of explorers, pioneers, men seeking riches to mine or farm. They entered the wilds and there many remained, lost forever in a wilderness they could never out-muscle.

Next came loggers with new ways to perish, crushed beneath falling branches, cleaved by poorly aimed axes, haunted by the tales told around midnight campfires ... legends of Sasquatch and grizzlies and spirit wolves.

Now survivalists and isolationists had joined the fray, hoping for a future more to their liking, many willing to murder to get it. Marijuana growers were at war with pot pirates or anyone else who got in their way. Conservationists and hikers went astray until their bones resurfaced the next year or decade or never. Homeless families who had reached the absolute end of the line huddled together in treacherous camps.

"And now there's a new form of insanity," Shaylee muttered to herself. The message from First Female. And from Wren about their missing woman. "How the hell will we stop slavers?"

"What you talking about, boss?" Jamie asked. He'd come up behind her. She'd been so preoccupied that she hadn't heard him approach.

"Tell me what's buggin' you. I want to help," Jamie said. He was a big, strong logger, the newest on her crew. His hair glowed fire red. His freckles matched. At the moment, his teenage face was a picture of concern for the boss lady.

167

"Tell him, Shaylee." With no more warning than that, Cascadia de-energized her invisibility. She was there on the back of her war bear. While Blue was delighted to see his friend Silver Tip and nickered a greeting, the three mares shrieked in fear.

Despite turning ghost white at the sight of the spirit, Jamie attended to the horses, their hooves whistling close to his face. He shooshed and whoaed.

"Be still, horses. Silver Tip will not hurt you," Cascadia said to the Percherons. At her voice, they magically settled. She then turned to Jamie. "Nor shall we hurt you, young friend of Shaylee."

But Jamie had gone still, staring at her, mouth agape. At least he was still until he toppled over in a dead faint.

"Timber," said Shaylee, knowing she had some explaining to do.

* * *

Jamie awakened in the barn, slumped over a hay bale where Cascadia and Shaylee had moved him. Shaylee watched color return under the freckles across his nose and cheeks. Then she saw it drain again when he looked at Cascadia.

Shaylee saw a plain woman in a tie-dyed t-shirt with the saying *I'm Nacho Mama* and who seemed to be covered with a fine golden dust. Jamie obviously saw something quite different. Shock and awe chased across his face.

"Who? What?" he breathed.

"Jamie, this is Cascadia. She comes from another place to help me here."

Jamie rose up, wobbled a bit and approached Cascadia who was standing in front of the huge bear. It lifted a lip and huffed at him but made no move in his direction. The spirit was no taller than the boy's solar plexus. She said, "This is Silver Tip, who is to me as Blue is to Shaylee."

Silver Tip grunted at the comparison to a horse. Of course, he was fond of this particular horse. He ignored Jamie and swayed over to the Percheron for a good natter.

Jamie turned to Shaylee. "Who? What?" he repeated. He sat back down on the bale.

"Jamie, you already know I disappear into the woods every now and then. You've helped me pack up. And you've never asked."

"Not my business 'til you make it my business."

Shaylee wished she had revealed more. There was so much to tell him now. "I need your word that what we say here will remain secret. Tell me now if you don't want to hear about crime. And spirits. And flying bears."

Jamie looked from Shaylee to Cascadia and back. "I'm thinking danger is involved."

"Yes," said Shaylee.

"Yes," said Cascadia.

"But it's important?"

"Yes," said both.

He shrugged. "Then I'm in."

Shaylee knew Jamie was grateful to her for hiring him when teens, even big strong ones, had trouble finding work. The woods would have to wait for a while today. She retrieved a Thermos of coffee from her truck. Jamie and she shared the strong brew. Cascadia never partook of the odd smelling potion that humans used in their ritual to herald the new day.

"All right, then. There's two tales to tell. What I've been doing and what's happening now." Shaylee sat on another bale and explained. "Some of this is new to you, too, Cascadia."

"I am proud to be part of your human pack. Jamie is a very appealing and sweet man."

As the boy blushed, Shaylee explained, "Cascadia says what she thinks."

"This is wrong to say he is what humans call hot?"

"Not at all, not at all," Jamie beamed.

"Okay, settle down and listen up, both of you. I work with a group called Bird Woman. They save women from abusers and stalkers when the law can't help them. It's not always legal, and it's almost always dangerous. Want me to go on, or do you want out now?"

Jamie looked down at his enormous feet and kicked a dry manure clod off one steel toe of his Wolverine logger boots. "My Dad used to slap my Mom around. Before I got this big. Keep going."

"The law can't do a damn thing until a stalker actually lays hands on his prey. Maybe kills her."

"What about restraining orders?" Jamie asked.

"Restraining orders, hell. Might as well be toilet paper."

"Or that women's shelter in town?"

"Women's shelters help but most aren't staffed to handle extreme violence."

Shaylee told Jamie and Cascadia about Wren Grisholm and the Bird Woman compound. She described how, with Blue's help, she'd started by carrying supplies in her modified wagon out to the group. And how she'd become even more involved.

"Not all of the women can get to the camp. It's a long hike. Maybe they can't walk that far, or maybe they have little kids. Whatever, I transport them in the wagon sometimes along with supplies. Wren organizes it all." She explained that women stayed at Bird Woman until Wren could arrange for false IDs. The compound had been an abandoned homestead so they had room to raise a few crops and farm animals. There was a large enough clearing that Blake kept an old Cessna there. When the time was right, he flew a woman away. Nobody but he and Wren knew who went where.

"Blake?" Jamie asked.

"You'll meet him. Lives out there in the woods somewhere."

"Blake is Shaylee's lust partner."

Shaylee burned as Jamie laughed. "Gotta be honest, Boss. Jack and I been wondering. Most every man in River Junction's been wondering."

"You just keep it to yourself or you and Jack will both be looking for work."

"Yes, ma'am," he said, his eyes twinkling.

"Anyway, as I was saying. It's been working fine. Once in a while, we need to persuade a jerk wad to leave the women alone. Some guys can be particularly motivated to find their runaways. But we've handled the danger so far."

"Until now," said Cascadia.

"Yes. Now there's a new menace. It's a group of survivalists out there who've begun to take slaves from the other societies in the forest. From the homeless or the salal pickers. And now a young female from Bird Woman."

"They're making people slaves? That's revolting," Jamie said. "Damn, I may pass out again."

"Wren is frantic to get Bonnie back before the bastards destroy her."

Jamie made a noise that was too low, too primal to be actual words.

Cascadia said, "I am to assess the type of warrior we need to create a horde of goodness who will take back the slaves and stop the aggression. First Female will provide this warrior from the Tree of Human History."

Shaylee understood she was to be the human commander of this mission, leading alongside her spirit advisor Cascadia. First Female had left her in no doubt of that. She might be asked to do things that the laws of nature would support but not the laws of the local sheriff. "Cascadia, my friend. I'm thinking we may need more than one warrior."

With that they talked strategies. And young Jamie Farrell became their first recruit in the Horde of Goodness.

CHAPTER FOURTEEN

The dusting of hope must be wearing thin. Cascadia felt an ominous chill from the wilderness speeding past below the flying bear. Rivers and ravines, mountains and coast held their breath and pulsed with threatening doom. Malevolence was in the air as any spirit worth the word could feel.

"Elpis believes the more hope the merrier. But in this, I fear the goddess may be wrong." Silver Tip aimed a huge teddy bear ear toward her then back to the skyway ahead. He was busy with navigation, happily contemplating the fish he planned to catch for dinner.

"Elpis put her very life on the line to save hope for humans. She nearly perished hanging on inside Pandora's jar when all else was lost. Is that why she cannot see that hope could become a blindness in itself? That too much of it might cause humans to take leave of their senses, become irrational in their beliefs?" This was complicated thinking for the spirit. She was used to trusting what her mentors said. But could gods be sometimes wrong?

Silver Tip didn't bother trying to understand her chatter. He was wondering how he could get her to gather moths for his dessert.

"Can I see what she cannot?" Cascadia whispered as though the words should not be expressed aloud.

"Am I coming to know more about humans than a goddess can teach me?"

Silver Tip flew on silently through the steel gray clouds. His job was to protect the spirit, not to understand her. She patted his head. "You are a good bear but a bear. I would like to discuss this with Shaylee." For the first time, Cascadia felt an unease with her mentors. She was growing into the very thing that First Female had created her to be. She was becoming a bridge between one world and another.

Like humans, she began to question the whys and wherefores. Her godly mentors knew exactly what to do; things were rarely so clear to humans. Their brains often made them question their capabilities. *Indecision and decision*. Maybe this was part of what it meant to be human.

Silver Tip plopped to earth and wandered away to their favorite pool as Cascadia called on Hammer to help her find Elpis. The pileated woodpecker answered with an earsplitting caw, then cocked his sleek head, listened to the wind and flew to a distant oak tree on the opposite side of a deep ravine. There he plucked an acorn and brought it back to Cascadia, dropping it in her hand. With another blast that hurt her ears at such close range, Hammer flew on his way. The messenger of the forest always had other tales to tattle.

Cascadia heard a faint sound of buzzing from the acorn. She held it to her ear then gave it a little jiggle. "Ooof!" it exclaimed. "Who's shaken me to waken me?" The lid popped up and out flew Elpis. "You dumped me on my butt, that's what," the fairy complained while rubbing her posterior. "You never know who's napping in a nut."

Elpis hovered before Cascadia's eyes like a hummingbird and stretched herself awake. The cap of the acorn clung to her yellow fluff of head feathers. "Welcome back to you. We have much to do."

"Yes. Hostilities are coming to the forest. Even the ancient cedars shudder with doom."

"I, Hope, shall help humans cope."

"Shaylee is prepared to lead the Horde of Goodness." Cascadia shared with Elpis the requirements that her familiar and she had developed for an additional warrior or two, experienced in fighting the good fight in other wars, passed or yet to be.

When the spirit was finished, Elpis said, "Enough with the blather. I have warriors to gather. I fly to the Tree of Human History on a manhunt for combatants. You and Shaylee gather yours, two leggers and all fours. We meet at Bird Woman two human nights from now. Ciao!"

Cascadia watched as Elpis flew away. "Be safe, Elpis. You are the thing with feathers, quite fragile after all."

* * *

"I'm not getting on the back of that bear." Aiyana's jaw jutted forward, her lips turned down, her brows knit. She pointed at her own face. "See this expression? Humans call this a game face. It's a look of determination. In this case it means, 'Hell no, I won't go.'"

175

Cascadia tucked that information away, but she simply could not understand why Aiyana would not enjoy such a pleasant way to travel as bear back riding. "But you must, Aiyana, and bring with you your bag of magic."

"I won't bring my unguents and weeds, I won't be a party to battle. I'm stamping my foot now." And she did.

Cascadia wondered if that was how humans thumped like rabbits and why. She raised her voice as she'd heard them do when making a point. "You are the human healer. Your skills will be needed."

"Quit wheedling. I've had my fill of trying to heal the human condition. I live way the hell out here just to avoid this kind of crap."

"But way-the-hell-out-here is where danger is brewing. You should not be alone in the coming thunder. You must gather with others in the Horde of Goodness."

"Horde of Goodness?" The healer snorted at the phrase. "Horde of Goodness?"

"Yes, Aiyana. Spirits live but humans can die. I have seen this happen. I can not abide to see you slain. So we must stay together."

Aiyana added a squint to her facial gymnastics. "Are those damn goddesses teaching you how to manipulate?"

Cascadia didn't know what that meant, but another thought occurred to her. Maybe it would work on the stubborn healer. "Elpis promises you an assistant. You will like that. Someone to order around."

"Then let the assistant tend to the wounds. There. That's my first and last order."

Cascadia had not faced such belligerence in a human loved one before, only in Silver Tip. "I do not think this herbal assistant can be left to her own devices. She is not a good Presence. Elpis says her herbology is toxicology."

Aiyana's expression morphed to surprise. "You mean the gods are providing a *poisoner*? A de Medici, a Claudius, a Dr. Crippen? Someone to kill with a kindly cup of tea? The jab of an umbrella? A venomous drizzle into the ear?" Aiyana flapped her arms like the wings of a violent hen.

Silver Tip, fond of the healer for fixing his paw, choose not to growl but merely ducked out of the way as she flailed. He wondered if his feelings should be hurt by her reluctance to board his back. Whatever.

"Elpis feared you might refuse. She instructed me to tell you this is the ancient who adds speed to the working of weeds."

Aiyanna blanched. Her arms slowly lowered and her shoulders drooped. "They're calling up the Catalyst. This is bad."

Cascadia didn't follow but she decided it didn't matter when Aiyanna finally gave in. "I'll get my bag. You convince the bear to carry two. He'll have to kneel so I can climb aboard."

* * *

Shaylee and Jamie hiked behind the wagon as Blue pulled it toward the Bird Woman compound. They had loaded provisions for a long stay. Loosely covered by a tarp was a selection of weaponry.

"What did you tell Jack?" Jamie asked. Jack Bergstrom was the third member of their logging crew. "He's gonna wonder why we're not working."

"Told him I needed a week of R and R and that you were using the time to visit distant relatives."

"Did he buy it?"

"I doubt it. He's clever when he's not dumb bellied," she said using the old logger's term for drunk. "But ever since he met Cascadia he asks a lot fewer questions."

"I get that. She's a lot to ... think about."

They walked in the company of birdsong and rustling branches for a time. In a distant meadow a bull elk bugled his long eerie challenge. It was a sound so wild it never failed to give Shaylee goose bumps.

Jamie broke the human silence. "You know all kinds of groups live out here. Homeless, dopers, pickers. Are they all our targets?"

"Nope. Just the slavers. At least for now."

"Who are they?"

"Started as a group of survivalists. Mostly men, some women. Tough, secretive but okay, I guess, unless you crossed them. A lot of isolationists are like that. Just want left alone. But this group not only wants to live its own way but force it on others, too."

"What happened to them?"

"Time maybe. Too much work. Clearing land is a bitch. People have turned to slaves for centuries to do the heavy lifting."

"But how dare they?"

"Belief that they're the only law of the land out here? Newer, darker leadership? I don't know. Wren can tell us more when we get to the compound."

They arrived at the creek that had been on the rampage the day Shaylee met Cascadia. She told Jamie about the near calamity as they clambered into the wagon. Blue picked his way up the creek bed, this time with ease. He lifted his knees high then splashed down his enormous hooves as though trying to soak his passengers.

Jamie finally blurted out, "I gotta ask. Why is Cascadia always dressed like she's in a *Sports Illustrated* swimsuit issue?"

Shaylee couldn't help but laugh. "She isn't. She wears shorts and t-shirts. When she flew in to tell us to go to Bird Woman, *I Let the Dogs Out* was printed across her chest."

"I'm pretty sure that's not what I saw on her chest," Jamie observed.

"A women sees what Cascadia actually is. A man sees his fantasy. It's magic she got from Helen of Troy."

Jamie sighed. "About the time I think I'm getting a handle on female behavior, something like this happens."

"Don't think you'll ever get the handle on female behavior," said the tall man who appeared on the bank as Blue was pulling the wagon out of the creek. A coydog stood tense behind him, ready to scurry into the cover of the trees.

"Baloney, Blake," said Shaylee, slipping out of the wagon and onto the rocky ground. "I'm an open book."

"Right. An unusual woman in many ways."

She smiled and opened her arms to him. Blake planted a kiss on her that knocked the scrunchie clear out of her hair. Her curls burst free in a joyful dance. When Blake released her, she sighed deeply then said to Jamie, "There. That'll give you and Jack something to talk about."

She introduced them, and the three continued on their way. With her loyal employee on one side and her lust partner on the other, not to mention the horse ahead of her and the coydog scouting the distant terrain, Shaylee felt safe from harm.

But she knew that safety was a mirage. Bonnie, the woman abducted from Bird Woman, was proof enough of that. She had been freed from her stalker only to find herself taken by a group of survivalists. Enslaved. Chained. Underfed. Beaten. Shaylee's mind ran wild with the dreadful things that could befall the woman. Each day that passed would be worse for her with no safety in sight.

Shaylee had felt that kind of hopelessness as a child, holed up in the barn or the corn crib. Hide and seek. She'd always been found by her uncle or cousin, and it was always horrible. Only the intervention of First Female had saved her. Maybe Bonnie could be brought back from the edge as well. But to save her, it would have to be soon.

Shadow's howl of alarm in the near distance shook Shaylee from her reverie. Blue snorted and froze in his tracks, head raised, ears at attention.

"Something's up there, around that bend," Blake said. He took his rifle from its sling and held it at his side.

Jamie stood next to the weapons in the wagon and Shaylee called, "Who's there?" She grabbed a logging chain, clutched it in both hands and swung the massive hook on one end slowly back and forth. Menacing, daring danger to show itself.

Three men and a woman materialized on the trail in front of them. Mutterings of *mierda* and *chingado* came from their pack. They shared pitch black hair, copper skin, and raised machetes.

"No problema, senorita y senores," said the leader, lowering his knife and setting down the bundle of greenery he carried on his back. The others held on to their loads. He switched to broken English. "We scare you. But you scare us, *tambien.*"

"Who are you?" Blake asked.

As her heartbeat slowed, Shaylee realized they were brush-pickers who gathered wild – and often illegal – harvests. Looked like they were after salal today.

"We are what you call pickers," the leader confirmed.

"You have permits?" Blake asked.

The workers' sullen glances at each other were answer enough.

Blake put his rifle back in its sling. "You guys had any trouble out here? Anyone been attacking your crews?"

None answered.

"We've heard stories of people being kidnapped."

The leader, the one who spoke English, translated for the others. A couple argued with each other and then with him until he shut them down.

Shaylee suspected the pickers had been attacked from their urgent chatter, but she figured they wouldn't tell tales. Jamie, Blake and she should keep quiet, too, what with planning a conflict and all. She stepped in and said, "Okay, you go on your way and so will we. We'll tell no one about you."

The group leader peered at her then nodded. He picked up his load and the little group passed by the wagon, disappearing down the trail as quietly as they had appeared.

"Will they circle back? Are they dangerous?" Jamie asked.

"Drug runners are. But these guys? Probably not to us. Some bash each other to steal harvests." Blake paused and looked at Shaylee. "Shaylee? You can probably put that chain away now."

She hadn't realized she was still brandishing the logging-tool-cum-weapon. With a shrug of her shoulders she returned it to the wagon.

They continued on their way until the forest grew thicker and their path narrowed to a tunnel bored through a dense tangle. Finally Blake said to Jamie, "Take a close look at the deadfall ahead. It's like one of those illusionary posters. Stare long enough and a second image will appear."

The kid squinted at the thorny blackberry thickets and snarls of vine maple and ivy. After a moment he gasped. "It's a fence!"

"It's Bird Woman," Shaylee confirmed. "They built a wattle fence from green saplings woven through posts. Like a huge basket. Once the saplings dry, it's strong as iron. And see these?" She indicated branch ends throughout the barricade which had been honed to sharp points with hatchets. "Not too comfy to climb over ... and the camp sentinels would hear anyone try to cut through it."

"Like stalkers, you mean."

Shaylee nodded. "There's only one break in the barricade wide enough for a horse Blue's size. Come on."

The entrance was a series of zigzags with no sightline straight ahead. When the compound revealed itself, Jamie breathed, "Holy crap. It's big."

An open area was dotted with buildings and an orchard planted by a homesick farmer's wife many decades before. Chickens, pygmy goats and two dairy cows ranged around the meadow at will. An old Cessna was tied down beside a grassy airstrip.

Shaylee said to Jamie, "When Wren Grisholm started this place, she thought all the women would move on. But several stayed. They've made it their home. Here she comes now."

As they awaited a woman walking from the house toward them, Blake said, "They gutted the original farmhouse and added bedrooms. It's like a small sorority house now. Or so I'm told."

Shaylee said, "Wren owns it. She's a descendant of the family who settled here. She has native blood, too, but there's enough Grisholm blood in her veins that she inherited the land."

"Wren is entirely too sweet a name for her," Blake added. Shaylee saw from his grin that he was well aware the woman was close enough now to overhear. "Shrike maybe. Or Raptor. Watch yourself, Jamie. She's especially tough on men."

"It's been our experience that is as it should be," Wren said. "Men are not allowed in our main buildings. You camp over there with the rest of your combatants." She pointed to the distant end of the clearing.

"The rest of our combatants?"

"Strangers have been arriving, asking for you, Shaylee. Very strange strangers."

A bellow from the distance interrupted them. "Been blinding any more Bulgars, you bloody Byzantine?" Metal clashed against metal.

Wren shook her head. "Go settle that. Then come tell me what the fuck's afoot in the forest."

* * *

"Have you run out of brothers to murder? Taste my sword, you louse-infested Norseman." One thrust and the other ducked.

Shaylee, Blake and Jamie arrived at the far end of the meadow in time to see two enormous thugs circling each other. One was clad in thick furs and a helmet studded with auroch horns. He wielded a

184

double headed axe, slashing it back and forth in front of him. The other, in colorful flowing robes and a golden crown, held a body shield along with his broad bladed weapon. Both smelled of sweat and seriously dirty laundry.

"What the hell?" asked Jamie.

"Who the hell?" asked Shaylee.

"How the hell?" asked Blake, pulling the rifle from its scabbard and taking aim. "Hey, you two, knock it off."

The combatants stopped circling. They turned to the newcomers. Drops of blood and spittle accompanied the swing of their heads. "You will conquer us with a stick?" sneered one.

"Sansorðinn," scoffed the other.

Shaylee figured the word didn't mean welcome. She looked from the warriors to the rifle. "A *stick*? Where did these two come from?"

"When are they from?" Jamie's question sounded pinched since he was holding his nose to ward off the stench of rot.

"I am Erik Bloodaxe, Viking lord of all I survey."

"It is I, Basil the Bulgar-Slayer, who rules the world."

"By torturing his own."

"By rape and pillage."

The two turned back to each other, posturing and circling once more.

Cascadia chose that moment to de-energize her invisibility. She appeared on the back of Silver Tip in mid-roar. The spirit swung her magic Web of Revenge and released it over the two warriors. They drew together swift as magnets, mashed nose to nose and axe to sword.

"Quiet, you two," the spirit commanded and her war bear growled a warning that caused them to lower their cursing.

"Awesome," muttered Jamie.

"Greetings, Horde of Goodness," Cascadia said to the three modern humans. "These ancient warriors have been called up by Elpis to aid in our attack on badness."

"Ah, I have a hunch these two are the very essence of badness," Blake said to Shaylee.

Meanwhile, an angry voice yelled, "Let me off this ursine whirlwind." Silver Tip kneeled and a woman, carrying a large woven bag, slid from behind Cascadia to the ground. She straightened her skirt and dusted off her sleeves.

Shaylee was perplexed, but that must wait. First things first. "Um, Cascadia? I believe a mistake may have been made. I know we need combatants. But more in the line of strategists, I think, than actual barbarian battle makers."

"Oh." Cascadia pulled what appeared to be an acorn from her pocket and consulted it. She held it to her ear. Within seconds the two warriors – who had taken to biting each other even though the net stung and constricted them – vanished.

When they were gone, it seemed unnaturally quiet. Shaylee could use a normal tone of voice. "We need someone used to surviving in a forest. Knows when to hide in the trees and when to use deception. A stealthy soldier. Maybe even a point man."

186

From the hemlocks and firs that rimmed the meadow, a presence stepped forth. "You called?" asked Sasquatch.

CHAPTER FIFTEEN

By evening, everyone gathered around a camp fire. They had been fed by the women of the camp, a feast of smoked trout, camas root and sweet wild huckleberries in heavy cream. Most of them had refused to try the skunk cabbage conglomeration that was a favorite of Wren's Clackamas ancestors.

"Tastes worse than it smells, and it smells like rot," Blake whispered to Shaylee after he ventured a bite.

Of the humans, only Blake had actually seen Sasquatch before and then only a fleeting glance as the creature dispersed like smoke in the wind. Shaylee realized that Cascadia accepted Sasquatch as one of many paranormal presences in her life. And Jamie seemed to believe that once the weirdness had begun, anything could happen. He seemed to be delighted as if starring in a marvelous sci fi movie.

But Shaylee felt dumbfounded. She'd heard the silly rumors and seen the ridiculous videos of Big Foot. Locals knew it was just a myth meant to draw cash out of tourist wallets in return for key chains, magnets and other trinkets laden with footprints.

Now it's real. I'll be damned.

Even though they'd met hours before, Shaylee still couldn't help but stare. Sasquatch was as tall as a fur-bearing streetlight, slender as a reed, rare as a genocide survivor. Yes, his feet were big. That was to be expected. But the beads around his neck, the feathered headband, the fact that he talked like an old hippie? That was some mighty surprising bullshit.

"Dudes," he'd said during introductions. "Call me Sas. Can you dig it? Flower children found me and grew me up decades ago. The Skookum, Willapa and others in these forests think I'm from some ancient native tribe of seriously ugly giants." With that, he took a toke from a fat doobie. "Far out."

Shaylee thought the Cascadian tribes might be right. Giants figured into most of their mythologies.

"Man, it's a drag for me to stay hidden," Sas said, pausing to scratch his chest. "Now you freaks come here talkin' violence in my backyard? Blows my mind. Gotta get that shit stopped fast. Kick the bastards out of Dodge and board the magic bus back to groovy town."

"What language does he speak?" asked Cascadia, looking to Shaylee.

"He's going to lead us into battle. At least I think," Shaylee translated.

"Lead? No way Jose." This time Sas gave a shake of his head so vigorous that a puff of no-see-ums took flight from his fur. "Ain't me, babe. I go with the flow. I lay it out, you deadheads act it out."

"Ummm ... so you're here to point stuff out, not join in?" Shaylee asked.

"Something wrong with your ear holes, little girl? I make love not war. Like I said to First Female when she recruited me. The only explosives I use are the mind-altering kind."

189

Shaylee sighed. If Sasquatch had managed to stay hidden for so many decades then he was a likely candidate to be seen, not heard. He'd be a good scout but probably no more than that. He was a pacifist not geared to hurting a soul even though the look of him could probably stop Eric Bloodaxe's blood in its tracks.

Shaylee's attention touched down back in the present. The campfire was warm, her belly was full, Blake was a fist bump away. Cascadia was passing an octagonal hatbox from person to Sasquatch to person. "Elpis has provided each of us with a lid to remind us of who we are. Take one and wear it."

Jamie picked a ball cap out of the box. It was covered with a dusting of gold. He studied the logo on the front and knit his eyebrows. "HOG?"

Blake followed. "We're HOGs?"

"Elpis says it is the symbol for Horde of Goodness. Those who wear these lids will always have hope." She squeezed her eyes shut as though extracting a memory. "She said 'Don't frown. Put HOG on your crown and I'll always be around.'"

"Who's Elpis?" Jamie asked looking around for someone new.

"The Goddess of Hope, of course," Cascadia answered. "She'll be here when we need her."

"Yeah, right," he chuckled. "Another goddess. Sure."

Shaylee, Cascadia, Jamie, Blake, Sas, Wren and Aiyana all put the caps on their heads. On Sas, it perched with a precarious wobble. Golden dust powdered their shoulders. Shaylee could tell a feeling of pleasure and a bond of trust was sprinkling them all.

The HOGs had Hope.

"Now that's a fine high, fellow freaks," crooned Sas.

As the campfire crackled, Wren told them more about their enemy. "They're survivalists. This particular group has been in the woods a long time. In the early days, it was about living on the land and forming their own civilization. Nothing wrong with that." She stopped to stir up the fire then continued the story. "Now it's a lot more militaristic. Kind of a cult, I guess. Anti-government. Anti-everyone else in the woods. They poach wildlife, steal plants, take from other groups. Members kowtow to their leader now."

"Who is he?" Shaylee asked.

"He's not a *he*," Wren said. "He's a she. Calls herself Scorn. Like hell hath no fury and all of that. It's my fault, I guess."

Sas cut in. "I've heard of her. She's some righteous cruel chick."

Shaylee asked Wren, "How is it your fault?"

"She used to be here at Bird Woman. I taught her how to get by in the woods, how to fend for herself and defend herself. She got strong, was a good deputy for me when I was busy elsewhere. You knew her, Blake. Her name was Catherine Grimes back then."

"Catherine! I wondered what became of her when you didn't have me fly her out of here. I liked her."

Shaylee wondered how much he had liked her.

"I liked her, too," Wren said. "She stayed with us because she was happy here. She was a natural at this life. Cunning, brave. Understood the forest. But the day came when she wanted me to lead a group to the city, find the man who had stalked her and murder him. I said no, that as long as she was safe from him, he was safe from us. I told her we only kept secure out here by staying off the grid, under the radar of civilization."

"I take it she didn't take no for an answer," Shaylee said.

Wren shook her head. "Nope. She said she understood. But she went back and murdered him herself with the new-found self-reliance she had learned from me."

"That's one fucked up skirt," Sas added. The sweet aroma of his weed enriched the smoke from the fire and enhanced the dusting of hope. He was so mellow he'd relaxed into a boneless pile of fur.

Wren took a sip of wine then nodded. "It was messy. She covered her trail but she could have blown our cover. Catherine thought she could stay here after that. But I kicked her out. We're a cult of sorts ourselves, you know. Everyone has to follow the rules. She packed up her skills and went to join the survivalists. Eventually she reappeared as Scorn. Introduced the idea of slavery to them. Now she runs the show."

"How'd that happen? Why did it happen?"

"Why? I suppose because she's a woman abused by men then abandoned by a woman she trusted, namely me. Probably felt it was her turn to be on top.

192

Don't know about the *how*. But she's wily and skilled enough to succeed. She knows the work it takes to clear land, build a camp, maintain it against all odds. She knows where to find people who labor to make it work. At the homeless camp. Among the pickers. Here at Bird Woman. Hard workers. Good stock to take as slaves."

"That's vile," Jamie said.

Shaylee agreed but she got it. "Societies have built themselves on the backs of slave labor for centuries. Hard to put up a pyramid without them."

They talked deep into the night, making decisions, laying plans, dividing responsibility. Before morning, they all knew that Shaylee was leading the show. Blackness was giving way to gray and owls screeched their final calls when Shaylee finally stood and stretched. "First thing in the morning, we warn the potential victims in other groups. Then we go get the kidnapped back.

* * *

Day came early for the leader of the HOGs. Shaylee had slept little but there was much to do. "Having greatness thrust upon you is not all it's cracked up to be," she muttered to the universe as she untangled herself from a sleeping Blake, found her underwear and went in search of coffee. She saw two of the Bird Woman residents already at work in the garden, another milking goats and a fourth repairing a roof on a shed. Birds were welcoming the sun.

After a jaw-stretching yawn she muttered, "Morning brought to you by Disney," then entered the kitchen. Only Aiyana was there. Her shoulders were hunched and the skin around her eyes sagged. Gray tendrils had escaped the knot of hair at the back of her neck. She looked as though her best mornings were all behind her. Shaylee wondered if the upcoming clash might take too big a toll on the healer. When she broke into the woman's reverie with a cheery good morning, Aiyana even flinched.

"Sorry to startle you," Shaylee said, pouring herself a cup and joining the healer at a table.

"Not startled. Just making a mental list of herbs and unguents I'm likely to need."

"We had little chance to talk yesterday, but I am pleased to finally meet you," Shaylee said. "Cascadia has told me about you."

"Ditto, my dear. Being her familiar, well, it can't always be easy."

"Not always easy, but always enlightening."

"It pleases me that easy is not an essential in our friendship," Cascadia said materializing in the third chair at the table. "It is also pleasing to see you speak with each other, even over this loathsome brew you humans share."

"You have to stop showing up like that." Aiyana snapped. "Or your *I Survived Shit Creek* t-shirt will say that you didn't survive me."

Shaylee laughed, but Cascadia ignored the healer's pique, saying, "Since I am always enlightening, Shaylee, I am here to tell you that Aiyana is worried."

"No secrets around here," Shaylee said. Her smile disappeared. "What's up, Aiyana?"

194

The healer cast a gloomy look at the familiar. "You will fight, all of you. Bravely. You will have wounds, and I will be there to heal the ones that are in my power. But I am worried about the entity who will be with us on the battlefield."

"She says it's a cat," Cascadia said.

"A cat?" Shaylee envisioned a goddess created hellion with saber teeth, nine vicious lives and no mercy as it spit acidic hairballs at the horde.

"Not a cat. A catalyst," Aiyana clarified. "Her name is Achlys. She's one of First Female's least charming nasties. My medicines will heal. Hers will kill. If I try to save, she may prematurely release the Death Mist that spreads across our eyes at life's end."

Shaylee protested. "But surely First Female would not send us such a wraith. Why would she?"

"Because she knows I won't kill when our adversaries fall. I'll try to save them, too. Achlys will do no such thing and will bar my efforts. Notice that First Female didn't introduce her directly to Cascadia."

"Why's that?" Shaylee asked.

"Because Nemesis has taught Cascadia justice. Achlys would teach her a thirst for carnage."

"I do not know this word, carnage," Cascadia said. The other two ignored her.

"The Keeper of the Death Mist. She's hazardous waste, Shaylee. Probably worse than the survivalists."

Shaylee exhaled a low whistle. "A woman named Scorn was bad enough. Now the Death Mist? Cripes. Could things get any harder?"

The screen door squeaked open and they looked up. Blake, not allowed to enter the building, leaned in. "The rest of the HOGs have assembled, ladies. We're waiting for our assignments."

* * *

Shaylee went outside and greeted the HOGs in the meadow. She took inventory.

Humans: A woman who hid women, a boy who cut trees, a man who knew military moves.

Animals: An oversized horse, a flying bear, a coydog too nervous to come out of the woods.

Whatevers: A Sasquatch high on life, a spirit in cahoots with the so-far-unseen Goddess of Hope.

Sure. No problem to stop human trafficking with this bunch. Still, First Female chose me to lead so I'm by goddess gonna do it.

Shaylee gave herself the pep talk because, in general, she'd rather duck below notice than rise above it. The biggest crowd she'd ever commanded was her logging crew of two people and four horses. But she began with the confidence of General Patton. "There'll soon be a clash and we're in it. Our goal is to break up the survivalist camp and release any prisoners they hold. We will force the slavers out of the woods or, if need be, see they can't harm anyone ever again. Their choice."

She actually paced in a line in front of them until she noticed what she was doing. She felt like an idiot and came to a standstill. "We know they have scavenger parties picking off people because that's how they got the girl named Bonnie. They may have other patrols and spies. When the scuffle starts they'll scatter, so the woods will be spookier than ever."

Would General Patton say spooky?

"Perilous. More perilous than ever. That's why our first move is to warn others in the area to be on the alert."

She turned to Wren and Jamie with the first assignment. "Find the pickers we encountered yesterday, Jamie. They won't be too far and will recognize you." She turned to Wren. "Wren, tell them about the kidnap of Bonnie. I believe from the way they acted yesterday that they've lost someone, too."

"And if they have?" Wren asked.

"Then maybe they could provide us a soldier or two. If not they still need to be warned that danger is coming. Tell them we will let them know when it is time."

"Consider it done."

"We could take Blue," Jamie said. "He'd let us ride ... I think."

"No, I have another job for him."

"Right then," Wren said. "We'll be off."

Jamie lifted an arm.

"You have something to add, Jamie?" Shaylee asked. "You don't have to raise your hand."

"Well, there's a homeless camp out that way. Not so far into the woods. Families gathered together. Very vulnerable. Could we go there, too?"

"By all means. Scorn's people could easily terrorize that group. Nobody would notice a missing homeless man or woman."

"How will we communicate?" Wren asked as they turned to go.

"The sat phones might not work when you're on the move. But Cascadia will check on you now and then. You know ... invisibility. Flying bear. You won't see her coming. "

Jamie and Wren hustled away. The woman sizzled with as much energy as the boy. Jamie was strong and Wren was smart. It should be a good team. Shaylee hoped they'd be safe.

Next she called on the newest group member who was swaying to some beat only he heard. "Sas."

He stopped grooving and looked at her. "You bellowed, Mama?"

"I want you to go to the pot growers around the woods."

"Far out!" Sas came out of his fog enough to sound excited.

Even though it was legal to grow weed in Washington, it couldn't be harvested on federal land and growers were a little loose on the details. Besides, they were touchy about outsiders due to the pot pirates who stole from them. Shaylee figured Sas knew exactly where they were and was highly qualified to warn them. Maybe even get them to join in a joint venture against the survivalists.

Joint venture. Ha!

Blake drew the toughest assignment. He was to go to the survivalists and ask for admittance to their group. His military background would be an asset that Scorn would surely relish. Besides, Scorn and

Blake already knew each other. Blake could spin a good story about looking for her.

"I'm giving you a couple other gifts that should look attractive to Scorn. You will arrive with your own strong, able slave in tow."

"Oh? And who might that be?"

She curtsied and said, "Ta-Dah! Shaylee Slave Girl at your service."

"That could become one of my best fantasies, Shaylee. But really, it's dangerous."

"No more for you than for me." Even General Patton could not be more obstinate than Shaylee when she made up her mind.

Blake rolled his eyes. "Okay, Slave Girl. What's gift number two?"

"Blue, of course."

"Blue? He's a horse. How can he help us?"

"Your job is to put as many of their weapons out of action as you can. My job is to free their slaves. Blue will calm their horses when a coydog shows up to set them loose. We don't want the bastards to have a swift means of escape."

She turned to her bestie. "Cascadia, you are the messenger between all groups. Only you have the speed and invisibility to do it. And then when Scorn orders the survivalists to stop us all, it will be your ... ah ... unique skill that will distract the men."

Cascadia's face lit with understanding. "When they see me, they will see their lust objects come to life."

"If that won't buy us time, I don't know what will."

* * *

The others began their assignments leaving Cascadia momentarily alone. Elpis left her acorn and flew to Cascadia's HOG hat. "Your plan is underway, hooray!" she chirped as she perched, dangling her elfin feet over the bill. She looked down between them and into Cascadia's eyes. "Your combatants seem full of hope, even the one who is full of dope."

Cascadia looked up at Elpis whose face was upside down to her own. She had never before criticized a goddess but it was time to give it a try. "Endless hope seems a good thing to you, Elpis. But humans appear to be easily blinded. Too much hope can lead them to irrational thinking. I mean, fairies aren't always going to come out of nowhere to save them."

For the briefest of moments, Elpis pushed out her lips, which ballooned her already chubby pink cheeks. She scratched her head of downy yellow feathers. But that was as long as her indomitable spirit could stand to be repressed. She flew off the cap and fluttered close to Cascadia's nose.

"Yes, yes, I guess your insight may be right. Too much hope and they take leave of their senses. Join Moonies or elect loonies. What a mess that would be, now I see!"

"To believe that nothing can go wrong will make them less than cautious." Cascadia didn't know the word for lack of caution but she realized there must be one. People had words for lots of feelings, many diagonally opposed. Not long ago, she'd known none of them. Now she realized each emotion had an opposite. They were very complex things! She proclaimed, "I begin to understand human emotions. I *get* it."

"You do, woo-hoo! Still it is sad I must add a darker dust to my magic. Measure out a pinch of doubt. Their expectations must have moderations. There are times wherein hope doesn't win. "

CHAPTER SIXTEEN

Cascadia overflew Jamie and Wren who were searching for the pickers. They were not far from Bird Woman, but the spirit could see they were already being followed by a two person scouting party. Jamie, a strong young specimen, would be an especially good capture for the slavers at Scorn's camp. He would be well suited to building compounds and clearing land.

Cascadia did not warn the two HOGs of their stalkers. She didn't disturb them at all. They had an important task to do and must continue on their way. Instead she whispered into the great bear's ear.

"Hold on to my hat," Cascadia yelled to Elpis as she threw off invisibility, and Silver Tip plunged to earth. He landed with a thud on top of one stalker while Cascadia roped the other with her Web of Revenge.

"You did not actually have to land on him, you know," Cascadia chided as she dismounted. She poked the bear on the meaty shoulder. "Move."

Silver Tip lifted his great self off the man, who was now a seriously flattened corpse with innards oozing out from under. Cascadia exhaled noisily and said, "Death comes swiftly when a grizzly falls on you from the sky."

202

"Bear in the air! What a scare! I declare!" Elpis seemed overwrought with excitement, fanning the air in front of her face to create a breeze. "Bad asses beware!"

At the same time, the stalker in the net was shrieking. She was also twisting herself violently.

Cascadia called, "Hush and freeze. The web will not sting if you remain still."

The stalker froze. This warrior was no fool, and Cascadia admired her for it. "Good. I will deal with you when I have spoken to my bear."

"Snarf! Grrmph," Silver Tip answered. He cuffed the dead man's head. It took flight, landing in a clump of salal.

"Stop that, you bad, bad bear. Nemesis will surely make me pay for that."

"Ar, ar, ar." Silver Tip backed away then rolled on his back enjoying a good scratch after a fresh kill. Maybe Cascadia would rub his enormous belly.

But she didn't. Instead, she turned away and released the net from her captive. "Be smart and you survive," she warned. She brandished her Bowie knife in case the captive had any life left to her. Which she did.

Freed from the net, the woman sprang up and crouched. She had a gladiator's stance and wasted no time pleading for mercy or questioning what just happened. Instead, a military grade Glock 35 appeared in her hand. She released a round in Cascadia's direction.

Cascadia was no longer there. She was invisible once more. She figured the warrior would have seen no more than a flash of metal as the Bowie knife hit her mid throat. She died having never said a word.

"Woo! That's two!" Elpis fluttered back to Cascadia's hat.

Cascadia said a word, one that humans used for defecation. Nemesis might take this death out on her, too, although the goddess condoned self protection. It depended on how she chose to look at it. Justified homicide or no.

Cascadia stared at the body, thinking the woman had been a fine warrior. How had she become so twisted as to believe other humans should belong to her? Maybe Shaylee could have taught her otherwise. The spirit felt a sense of loss. How vast sorrow was. How many things could make her feel sad.

But Elpis wouldn't have it. The fairy patted herself down, scanned the carnage and shook a finger at the spirit. "See here, my dear. Slavery is as tragic as black magic. This war has just begun but the first round you have won. No time to blink or double think. You do what you must do."

Cascadia nodded. She called to Silver Tip and flew on, leaving the two human bodies for whatever scavengers passed this way.

***

"First blood has been drawn," Shaylee said to Blake as she rode behind him on Blue's broad back. She briefed him on Cascadia's status report. "Jamie and Wren have found the pickers and moved on to warn the homeless camp. But Cascadia had to deal with two people who were stalking them."

"Deal with?"

"Don't ask. Just remember that her bear is not only lethal, he has a sense of humor."

"If they were Scorn's people and she hasn't missed them yet, she soon will. I'd like to get to her camp before she senses something's wrong."

Shaylee Slave Girl had been enjoying the view of Blake's shoulders as they rose and fell while the horse picked his way over logs and around brambles. They were riding to the survivalists' camp. Shaylee scooched forward so she could wrap her arms around him and tuck in close. The feel of him was as tantalizing as the sight. Meanwhile, she spoke to Blue. "If you can find better hoofing on your own, youngster, speed is of the essence."

The horse began to trot. Blake said, "You two are getting more like Cascadia and Silver Tip every day."

Shaylee wondered if he thought that was a good thing. She leaned her cheek close to his ear.

"It's really happening, Blake. And people are already getting killed. I can see this will be a series of skirmishes. This is no easy eviction."

"What they're doing is wrong, Shaylee. They may even be taking more people than they can use. They may be selling them now."

"I know, and that's terrifying. But maybe it isn't up to me just because First Female says so. Maybe I should go to the cops."

Blake snorted. Blue cocked an ear to the sound and answered with a snort of his own. "Blue and I agree. Go to the cops and tell them what, exactly? About an invisible spirit with a flying bear? A sasquatch? And your human witnesses are a military man who isn't exactly on the side of the angels plus a woman who would deny everything to save the women she hides from their husbands. I'm thinking the cops would be eager to rush in."

"When you put it that way ..."

"Whoever or whatever the hell First Female is, she's right. You and your raggedy ass crew are the only hope for the societies out here."

They rode on in silence but Blake must have been mulling it over because he added with passionate heat, "Why can't others respect those who just want to be left alone?"

Neither human heard the woman approach. Nor did Blue. When she stepped out of the woods onto the trail just in front of them, they all reacted with a start. Blake tensed, Blue halted, and Shaylee, trying to see around Blake, uttered, "What the ... "

She was cut off by the woman who said, "I remember a time when you didn't want me to leave you alone, Blake. When you wanted me close."

Blue threw back his head and whinnied as she grabbed for his reins.

"Catherine," Blake answered. "Or should I say Scorn?"

* * *

Shaylee quickly looked down. She didn't know how a slave girl would behave, but she figured a face-searing, pissed-bitch glare wasn't advisable. Besides, she'd already seen enough of Scorn to know the woodland hellion was a stunner, even in fatigue pants and a tank top. Not just pretty but tall, statuesque, regal.

Dammit to hell.

Shaylee could feel her eyes turn green with jealousy. Had Blake pursued this woman? Had she pursued him?

Quit it. This is war. Get your head out of your asshole.

Blue pranced in place, unsure whether things were safe for horses what with a stranger invading his space. "I come bearing gifts," Blake said as he slid to the ground. He turned to Shaylee and gruffly ordered, "Stay there."

Slave girl, slave girl, slave girl. Obey, obey, obey.

Repeating the mantra in her head, Shaylee blushed in anger but stayed in place. Blake put his hand behind Blue's ear and patted. The horse took it as a sign of good intent and settled down.

"Gifts? Don't you realize we survivalists have everything we need?" Scorn's voice oozed with her namesake, rich with mockery.

"But I know how you like presents. I come to you with a muscular young slave as well as a splendid workhorse."

Scorn touched the soft skin of Blue's muzzle, reached up and stroked his cheek. "He is a handsome fellow," she purred. Shaylee suffered a stab of jealousy, this time as her horse nickered his pleasure at the caress.

Damn it, Blue. Bite her. Head butt her. I hate her!

Scorn next looked at Shaylee as though she were appraising tomatoes in a market. "A woman with possibilities. Have you plucked this fruit yourself, Blake?"

"Now Catherine. The slave is for work not play."

She laughed. "Of course she is. But come now, Blake. Nothing is free. What do you want for these gifts?" The word *gifts* dripped with sarcasm.

"I want to join your group."

Her surprise seemed real. "You? Man of the woods? The lone wolf who cannot be civilized?"

"I'm tired of being on my own." He put his hand on her shoulder. "I miss many things society has to offer."

You son-of-a-bitching dick-faced ...

"And why would we want you?" Scorn continued, apparently unaware of the heat radiating from the slave.

"I'm ex-military, I know weapons. I believe that if you don't take in this world then you get taken."

"Hmm. Well, maybe so, maybe not. But come with me. Let's talk more about the possibilities of ... merging."

They began to walk. Shaylee, on the back of the horse, could no longer hear the conversation. But Blake looked happy. He was acting, that was all.

Acting.

She became aware others were escorting them. When she looked back she saw that two men with guns had closed ranks behind them.

Her jealousy fled, chased away by high anxiety. She never would have believed she'd feel unsafe in the company of Blake and Blue. But this band of crazies could kill Blake ... enslave her forever ... work Blue to death ...

Stop! This is what we wanted, right?

They were on their way to the heart of their target.

* * *

When Cascadia next checked on Jamie and Wren, they were speaking with the salal pickers. From the air she could see their body English – well, maybe half of it was body Spanish. She hovered like a hawk on the hunt until the two parties shook hands and the HOGs went on their way, moving toward the homeless camp.

She liked these two. Wren was tough. Jamie was, too, but he was also loyal. He did whatever Shaylee asked of him. Cascadia was glad her familiar had found two men that she could trust. Blake and Jamie helped make up for the men of her past.

When Jamie and Wren were far enough away from the pickers to be heard no more, Cascadia appeared ahead of them. Both were startled by her arrival even though Silver Tip carefully landed in front of them instead of on top of them.

"You have that bear under control, right?" Wren asked, eyebrows raised.

"I do. Unless you try to hurt me."

Wren looked at Jamie and laughed. "Damn, there goes that plan."

He snickered, too.

Cascadia cocked her head. "This is humor? You make the gurgling sound of happy humans."

Jamie said, "Sometimes people say the opposite of what they mean when it's funny."

"No wonder the gods have a hard time understanding humans. You are strange creatures."

Wren answered, "Yes, yes we are. Of course, I'm not the one wearing the *I Shih Tzu Not* t-shirt." She made the gurgle sound again.

Cascadia returned to a subject she understood. "Tell me what I should report to Shaylee about the pickers."

Jamie told her the boss lady had been right. The slavers stole a man from the picker's group. "Those dudes are pissed. They want to help. They'll be in the woods around the compound when the fighting breaks out. Any camp member trying to go AWOL will be met with machetes."

Wren added, "They don't want the bastards on the loose when the fighting stops. Just makes the woods more dangerous for the peaceful groups."

Cascadia consulted an acorn then nodded.

"Tell them we will give each slave a yellow scarf so they won't be mistaken for AWOLs. Everyone needs to be careful not to confuse the two."

Cascadia bid them farewell and flew in the direction of Sasquatch. She was confused by this entity. Mutant? Monster? Thing? He didn't seem quite human what with all that hair nor did he appear to be an animal since he spoke in people words. Sas smelled far worse than other earthly things, he stuck firesticks into his mouth throughout the day, he walked in a loose-boned gait that he called truckin'. Could he defend himself much less someone else? Would he? The really confusing part was that Shaylee seemed to think he was useful. She had given him the important job of warning a volatile woodland society that war was on its way. Cascadia wondered what she was missing.

She saw the pot growers below before she located Sas. They were on the slope of a foothill and had planted their crop in rows between young firs, hoping to hide its presence from the air. Since the young trees were conical in shape, the marijuana still got sunlight but blended in with the other greenery.

Two men were visible in the growing area and four more at a small campfire. She scanned the near horizon but it took her time to locate Sas. He was hidden in the branches of an ancient madrone as relaxed as if he swung in a hammock. From that vantage point in the forest ringing the growing field, he could look down on the growers.

As she watched he tensed and was gone. Only the moving boughs gave a hint that he'd ever been there at all.

She was taken aback. Where had he gone? Then she saw him in the field squatting behind the small firs, looking toward the camp. An inhale later, he was at the campfire. He moved so fast, he couldn't be seen as he dashed from place to place. Who'd have guessed it? The beast seemed so slow as he trucked along, but he could move faster than light, faster even than Silver Tip. No wonder there were so few human sightings of a Sasquatch. Cascadia felt herself warm toward him. Maybe he'd be useful after all, pacifist or not.

The growers looked hostile at the appearance of Sas. Two wielded weapons. Cascadia prepared to step in by unfurling the Web of Revenge. But soon everyone calmed. Some of them seemed to have met him before. Sas and the men squatted on their haunches around the camp fire and began to talk, smoke, drink. And talk, smoke, drink until the moon was the only light. Cascadia and Silver Tip finally found a sheltered spot under a basalt outcropping to curl up and spend the night.

In the morning, the growers' tents buzzed like an aviary with their snoring. The spirit soon found Sasquatch's feet and legs sticking out one flap. Peeking inside, she saw his head pushed up against the other end, belching out great snorts and gulps. The air in the tent reeked with stale booze and farts of whatever a Sasquatch ate. She hastily withdrew.

"I guess he is alive," she muttered to Silver Tip who was pawing his snout. "But he smells like he is rotting." Since they hadn't killed him, the growers must have accepted him as a prime customer if nothing else. She assumed Sas would get his message of warning across. So Cascadia and Silver Tip flew away to check on Aiyana before locating Shaylee.

* * *

Slave girl, slave girl, slave girl. Obey, obey, obey.

Shaylee had been given to three other slave women to help prepare and serve an evening meal to the camp members. When they discovered how badly she cooked, they relegated her to scullery duty. She tended a fire to keep water boiling then used it to wash endless pots and utensils. Her hands and arms were roughened to bright red from the lye in the soap. She knew the small curls around her face would be kinking from the heat of the water and flames. Even

212

though the late afternoon was cool, sweat trickled down her forehead and threatened her eyes.

She was flabbergasted that the three other women worked with no restraints. Why didn't they run? Why didn't they take those kitchen knives and chop heads? She considered tossing the boiling water on two men who had called them words she'd only seen on graffiti-etched walls. But without knowledge of Blake's whereabouts she didn't dare do any such thing.

Obey, obey, obey.

The survival camp had been in the mountains for a long time. It was certainly not the only one. Isolationists of all types had set up societies. Bird Woman was an example of that. But to Shaylee's knowledge, this was the only compound that had decided on slavery as a tool for development. Scorn had introduced the concept to the people here. How damaged she must have been by her past to want others to suffer, too.

Shaylee eyed the camp's topography from where she scoured and scrubbed. It rose on a high angle up the slope of a ridge. It was an opening in the trees but not a gentle meadow for gardening like the one at Bird Woman. Instead it was an austere stretch of land leading upward to a fissure in the rock wall. From the activity around it, she believed it must be a cave, maybe the central housing for camp members. Nothing could approach it without being seen. Shaylee heard the gurgle of a quick moving creek. Clean water and a cave safe from weather or invaders.

Lower on the slope, she saw a couple structures, some sort of home built quonsets. Like half pipes covered in camo. An armory? Showers? Stable?

The slave women had stationed her just outside the cookhouse for her scullery duties. It was a cedar structure with wood and propane stoves as well as a cooler running on a propane tank. Shelves were stocked with bags of grain, aseptic boxes, restaurant-sized canned goods. A row of picnic tables ran along one wall. Screens around the structure walls allowed air to circulate through it, but Shaylee saw wooden panels that could be dropped from the outside to close it against wet weather. She had seen maybe two dozen people as they came and went. She had no idea if everyone living in the camp came to the cookhouse to get their meals but it seemed a reasonable assumption.

Shaylee could hear animals, too. A rooster, the occasional bark, bray and whiney. She wondered if Blue had been given evening grain. Was he okay? Was Blake?

At the end of the meal, the women cleaned picnic tables and gathered the scraps and leftovers together on a large tray.

"For the dogs?" Shaylee asked.

"No, for us," one of them answered.

A guard walked them to one of the quonsets. He unlocked the door and ushered them in. Shaylee stood back to allow those carrying the tray and a bucket of fresh water to enter first. The guard grabbed her arm hard. "I'm told you're property of the new guy. We'll see about that." He let her go but not before pinching one of her breasts. It was meant to hurt, and it did. She gasped as he shoved her through the entrance and slammed a door behind her. She heard a bolt push home from the outside.

It was dim. The only light came from small window vents near the tops of the end walls. After sundown, it would be total darkness. As her eyes adjusted, Shaylee saw that three men were already in the space. From the women's greetings to them, Shaylee realized they were slaves, too. While the women made the meal, they must have had some other work detail.

All six sat on the floor around the tray and ate. Their only utensil was a ladle for the water bucket and they passed it around. They were dirty, bruised, tattered, but both the men and women appeared fit. None looked older than forty. Most were a lot younger.

One man tugged at her pant leg. "Sit. Eat."

"I'll sit," she said crossing her legs and slowly lowering herself to the floor with the rest of them. "But I can't eat."

"Maybe not yet. But you will." He turned back to the tray and took a wad of cold rice with his fingers.

Shaylee scanned the women. She'd had no chance to talk during the work shift about anything but dinner prep. "Is one of you Bonnie?"

No answer.

Shaylee tried again. "I've come from Bird Woman to find you."

Finally one of the women spoke. "A favorite hunting ground for these bastards. I'm Bonnie."

215

Shaylee introduced herself to all six of the slaves. She said she was there to help them get away. Their only response was a dazed stare.

What the hell? Why aren't they excited?

"My friends and I will get us all out of here."

Still no reaction.

"Are you too tired to hear this good news?"

"No. Too smart to react," said one of the men.

"I don't understand," Shaylee said in frustration.

Quiet. Then one spoke. It opened the floodgates and they all had something to say.

"We buried the last person who tried to escape."

"They made him watch while we dug his grave."

"He was alive when we watched them chop him apart. I still hear him screaming in my head."

"Each of us had to carry a bloody piece of him to the grave."

"Makes you less interested in escaping when you've seen something like that. Done something like that."

"It gets worse. If we give them too much trouble, they sell us. We're told a future like that is worse than this. And I believe it."

"As long as we work, they keep us fed, clothed. Such as it is."

"You're not the first to think you can get out. You won't be the last."

"So fuck you and your escape. This is the end of the road, girlie."

Shaylee felt sick at heart. The idea that the slaves would not help had never dawned on her.

Only Bonnie spoke to her after that. The men went to cots at one end of the building and the women to the other. Bonnie pointed out buckets behind a ragged curtain. She called them the facilities.

Shaylee set up a rickety cot and lowered herself onto it. She was exhausted but knew that sleep would not come to her. "Nice time to remain quiet," she muttered to First Female. Where the hell was a goddess when you needed one?

This was a place that had abandoned all hope. This was hell.

* * *

In the morning, Blake and Scorn were waiting for her outside the quonset. As the other slaves moved away, Scorn told her to wait.

Shaylee ached from a sleepless night on the cot, feared what the day would hold, smelled her own sweat, itched with dirt and had a belly ache from hunger. Blake looked fresh, composed and even dared to smile at her. How had he spent his night? Clearly, her role as slave was more strenuous than his as, what? New group member had been the goal. But was he also a new lover? Amidst the exhaustion, dirt, hunger, and fear, jealousy once again worked its vile way onto her list of woes.

"I'm told you are worthless in the kitchen for anything but scut work," Scorn said. "But you look strong. Blake says you and his horse are loggers."

HIS horse? Blue? HIS horse?

"If so, we have use for you both. Our last workhorse died. Come."

Shaylee followed them to a lean-to where Blue was tied next to two riding horses. Another horse and two mules were in an adjacent corral. Blue turned his head toward the humans and when he saw Shaylee, he whinnied and pawed the earth with a massive front hoof.

"He lets me get near him, but nobody else," Blake said. "And I can't harness him."

Scorn pointed out a pile of leather straps. "Get him ready. You'll work with three of our men clearing today. You may belong to Blake, but you will answer to anyone giving an order. You touch none of the saws, use nothing as a weapon. If you do, the horse will suffer the consequences."

Fear for Blue overtook all other emotion. Scorn knew how to go for the jugular.

"Do you understand, slave?"

I understand, you miserable hag. Touch MY horse and I will kill you.

"Yes. I understand."

"Good. Get him ready. Come Blake, I'll show you the compound and get you on our assignment schedule. Something with security, I should imagine."

Scorn linked her arm through Blake's and they walked away. Shaylee went to Blue. She leaned into his neck. He nickered a comforting welcome.

"Blue," she said, then reviewed the pile of leather. It was an old harness but serviceable. The horse collar was not a perfect fit, but she found some rags in the lean-to and padded it as best she could. "We're both gonna have to work hard today, big guy," she said as she fastened the buckles and leads.

218

"That's a fact, slave," said a voice behind her. She stiffened and turned to look. It was the man who had grabbed her breast the night before. "I'm Crew Boss today. Scorn says she'd punish the horse. But I'd punish you." He paused to smile broadly. "I look forward to it. The new guy isn't the only one who'll hear you moan. Now bring the horse and follow me."

Crew Boss wanted to hurt her. Like Uncle Carson had wanted to hurt her. And cousin Chad. They didn't cared about the fear and pain it brought to her. In Shaylee's mind they became one and the same. Her belief that there was good in everybody now seemed pathetic in its innocence. This kind of man would never change.

Crew Boss was going to die. She followed him into the woods, quietly planning as she lead the enormous horse. The morning mist gave way to rain.

CHAPTER SEVENTEEN

Silver Tip was grouchy. He was a mighty flying bear, for the love of goddess. The only fun he'd been allowed was one brief at-bat with a human head before the spirit had moved him on. She could be a real bear-buster. He wanted something to sink his teeth into. Or his claws.

Instead, here he was flying back and forth between humans, like some kind of taxi service. All this to-ing and fro-ing was boring. What was for lunch? When was this much ballyhooed battle going to begin?

Cascadia knew Silver Tip was feeling pissy. His flight was bumpier than necessary. Poor Elpis had shown signs of air sickness. "Dear girl, don't want to hurl on your chapeau, don't you know, so I think I'll go below." The fairy crawled off Cascadia's HOG hat and back into her acorn.

"See what you've done? Now behave," Cascadia said into the ursine ear. "When this is over, I will find you a honeycomb."

Silver Tip grunted and bucked.

"Okay then. I'll roll grubs in it."

The turbulence ended. Bribery worked for gods or humans or bears. She scratched the very top of his head as he smoothly whisked her back to Jamie and Wren.

The two HOGs were just leaving the homeless camp. It was a shabby tent city but not unclean. Families came and went as their fortunes rose and fell, but those who stayed made an effort at communal living. Cascadia had watched them from above before, men and women working in a garden and repairing tents, children wrestling with camp dogs or fishing the creek. To outsiders on a mission of human traffic, this group was very vulnerable.

This time when she landed in front of them, Wren and Jamie were ready for her appearance. "A couple went missing a month ago," Wren reported. "The group doesn't think they departed on their own accord. Left all their stuff behind, including their dog. The only reason they were out here instead of public housing was because they wouldn't get rid of the pooch."

Jamie summed it up. "The survivalists struck again."

Wren said, "These people have no fighters to add to our army. But they gave me this." She handed a bedraggled paper bag to Cascadia. "Lots of them have been prescribed meds that they won't take. Don't like the side effects. Thought you could give them to Aiyana in case injuries are beyond the help of her unguents."

"Where is Shaylee now?" Jamie asked. "Is the boss lady okay?"

"She is a slave. Blake is with Scorn. They have infiltrated the survivalist camp. It is dangerous for both now. The conflict starts soon."

* * *

"Steady. Watch your footing." Shaylee talked to Blue, urging him to take care as the fir needles, grit and wet earth turned to a slurry. They were both sweating in the rain, exhausted from the morning of enforced work with no break. Apparently, the survivalists needed more room. This hill, adjacent to the camp, was steep and nowhere near safe enough for logging with a horse, especially on ground as slick as a luge track.

Before they had begun she had told the Crew Boss as much. "It's too wet and too steep." He'd slapped her face and told her to fucking do what she was told. The rest of the crew had heard it all. Her smile was only inward.

They didn't know for sure, of course. This crew consisted of men with chainsaws. Only Shaylee was a logger. Years in the forest had taught her skills they would never know. Two of them were cutting far up the hill above her. Only Crew Boss was on the landing below, where she delivered the logs to the bottom of the hill. There he cut them into his desired length. He'd taken the easy job. And today, the dangerous one.

Blue had made many trips down the hill hauling a ton of timber every time. Shaylee made sure he used the same track with each trip. She danced from log to log to ground, testing every step. The racket from chainsaws above and the Crew Boss below covered any sound that she and her horse created.

When the earth and rain seemed right, she made her move. Blue's hooves had chopped the track, and run-off had done its job. If Shaylee waited any longer, the logs might avalanche catching the horse in their path. She stopped, adjusted the chain around the end of three mid-size logs, and rehooked it to the harness. Taking hold of Blue's bridle, Shaylee said, "Okay, Blue. I know this will seem weird. But come with me." Instead of continuing down, she turned the horse's head and led him to the side. As the logs resisted changing their course, his pull got harder. Blue didn't know this game but responded to the mystery. He snorted, lowered his head and gave a mighty heave.

The logs began to turn. And turn. They were no longer aimed down the slope but parallel to it, teetering sideways. Shaylee thought of those wobbling rocks in a road runner cartoon.

She backed the horse enough to release the hitch. The logs, now free on a wet slope, slowly began to slide. With a helping push from Shaylee, the pile moved off center, skidded faster and began to roll, one after another.

They picked up speed, knocking brush and saplings out of their way. The noise as they tumbled and crashed would have been warning but the chainsaws masked the sound.

When Shaylee reached the landing area at the bottom of the hill, she could tell that Crew Boss must have heard the pounding onslaught at the last second. He had turned in the direction of the log that hit him mid-chest. He'd seen death coming, had time to feel terror. Shaylee could see it on his face as she smiled down on the broken body. In her mind, Uncle Carson and Cousin Chad died with Crew Boss. At long last, she could heal the age-old wounds.

She moved fast then, grabbing handfuls of muck and covering Blue's right side with the needles, silt, and mud. His sweat and rain mixed in with the mess. Then she led him back up the slope to the crew still working at the top.

* * *

It had been close. Scorn was called, and Blake came with her. Shaylee told them how Blue had fallen on the slope and how she had unhooked the load so he could get free. And how the logs had begun to slide and the noise covered her screams of warning and what more could she do? The crew confirmed she had warned Crew Boss that it was too dangerous and he hadn't listened. The horse looked dirty enough to have fallen. Blake said his slave wasn't smart enough to concoct a story like this if it wasn't true.

Scorn frowned. She stared at Blake and then at Shaylee. Finally she shrugged. "He was an asshole. It couldn't be helped." To the crew she said, "Go bury the body. Take a couple slaves." To Shaylee she said, "Looks like you're back on scut work for now."

Shaylee had no idea if Scorn had bought the story or not.

* * *

Cascadia found Aiyana in the meadow at Bird Woman, gathering foxglove in a basket woven from bear grass leaves. The spirit handed the healer the

224

grubby bag of medicine. "These are from the homeless camp. The people there want to help if someone is injured when the battle begins."

Aiyana opened the bag, pulled out pill containers one by one, and read the labels. "Thoraxine ... droperidol ...loxapine ... Hell, Cascadia, these are all antipsychotics. Not an antibiotic or pain killer in the batch." Aiyana threw them back in the bag and closed it. "Of course, if anyone loses touch with reality in one form or another, we could medicate them. Since I think I'm speaking with a spirit maybe I should consider it."

"They are of no use?"

"Well ... if we dissolve them in the drinking water of a healthy enemy, we could create blurred vision, tremors and some really sleepless nights."

Cascadia said, "I believe we need stronger medicine than that." Then she looked skyward. It was a sound she knew well. She glanced at Aiyana, "Have I done wrong?"

"Wrong? Bringing me these things? No, but ..." Now Aiyana looked up, too, as the screech of the griffins stopped her comment. The beasts lowered their chariot to the meadow. Nemesis stepped out and a bent, skeletal figure in a dark cloak followed.

Aiyana gaped as Cascadia introduced the goddess.

"I know you, Aiyana. You are a good sort of human, though maligned by many."

"I know you, too, Nemesis. You are a good sort of goddess, though maligned by many."

They nearly smiled at each other.

Cascadia needed an answer now. "Have I displeased you, goddess? Have you come to punish me for Silver Tip's behavior? He did kill but only a human who might have killed him."

"No, spirit. Bears are judged on a different scale than humans, and not by me. I am here to bring you Achlys ... also known as Misery." Nemesis indicated the wraith who pulled back her hood revealing a pale emaciated face, a rictus grin of green teeth, and a dripping nose.

All three griffins hissed at her but she ignored them. "I am also called Eternal Night. Or if you prefer, Keeper of the Death Mist." Her words were spoken in a weeping voice not unlike the cry of loons.

"You are a pain in the ass and we don't need you here." Aiyana snarled with an aggression that Cascadia had not heard since they met over Silver Tip's injured paw.

"You would heal the wrong doer and let evil go free," wept Misery.

"You poison."

"You dabble."

"I do not kill."

"I do not save."

"Silence!" Nemesis brandished her scourge and even the griffins shut their beaks. "Salvation is your job on this earth, Healer. It is a human affair. But in the coming discord, you will not be allowed to help the bad ones. It has been ordained by First Female."

"Ha! The Death Mist comes for all." Misery gloated.

"Not in this clash, hag," Nemesis snapped. "I will judge the fairness of the death toll. It is my duty as adjudicator. We will see you in the combat zone."

And that was it. The gruesome goddesses returned to the chariot, the griffins lifted off, and they were gone.

Moments passed. Cascadia asked, "Achlys. She is the one you call the cat ... cat ..."

"Catalyst. Yes. Because she makes small wounds large, minor hurts major."

"Maybe she is the better medicine that we need."

"I have my doubts, little one. I have my doubts."

CHAPTER EIGHTEEN

That afternoon while scrubbing pots, Shaylee was awash in worry. She had not been able to talk with Blake or hear news of the HOGs and their progress. So she was enormously grateful when Cascadia's voice appeared near her ear. The spirit, wearing the cloak of invisibility, brought her familiar up to speed. She explained that the societies of the woods were ready. "I have also spoken with Hammer the woodpecker. He has gone to warn them with his mighty caws that the fracas will soon begin. When they hear, they will send warriors."

Shaylee could not speak aloud without fear of being overheard. But she knew that slaves often sang and thought it might be ignored by the camp tenders. Her knowledge of slave songs being what it was, she instead chose the tune of *I've Been Working on the Railroad* and warbled as best she could.

I've been working with the slaves,
All the live long day
Can't say they're exactly ready
To give their lives away.

"You sing?" Cascadia asked in surprise. "It is not good music but I get your meaning. Elpis will come to you tonight. She can be small and will enter the slave quonset through a chink I have found at the top of the wall. She is Hope. The slaves will respond. She will bring scarves they must wear."

Can you tell me if we're ready
To rise up early in the morn?
Can the man disable weapons
to start this war we've sworn?

Cascadia knit her brows then got it. "Ah! I go to Blake now. If he is ready, yes we can go in the morning. I will let you know."

Okay, let me know,
Okay, let me know,
Okay, let me know 'fore mooooorn
Okay, let me ...

"Stop that awful caterwauling," another kitchen slave yelled from the cookhouse. So Shaylee did. But she thought about the mission and how it was not one big battle but many small ones. Three survivalists were now dead, one by bear, one by Cascadia, one by Shaylee. It was a good start. But was the tide going to turn? If so, when? What would their losses be? She muttered a line she'd once heard attributed to General Patton. "Hope is a terrible battle plan."

But sometimes hope is all you have.

"Where is your ear?" Shaylee asked.

"I hear here," Cascadia answered. Shaylee felt Cascadia brush against her. "Please sing no more."

So Shaylee whispered her plan for the next morning.

* * *

Cascadia went on her way thinking she'd as soon hear a cow bellow as another note from Shaylee. When she found Blake, he seemed to be enjoying other members in the compound. She didn't understand the rules to poker but it involved gathering bits of cardboard in your hand, throwing them down with a swear word or two, and giving away your money. She waited, jumpy with nerves. If she'd known the word for it, she was suffering impatience.

Finally Blake stood, stretched and left for the one place a man goes to be alone. Cascadia followed him to the outhouse.

He was inside and she was outside, invisible to anyone who looked her way. "Blake?"

"Whoa! Is that you Cas ... ah, who's there?"

"Yes, Blake. I am outside your outhouse. We are alone."

"Ah, can you wait a minute? I won't be long."

"No. I have much to do."

"Well, I can't wait either. Apologies for the informalities. Is Shaylee okay?"

She heard the worry in his voice. "She is well unless she is singing." Cascadia gave him a full report, ending with the slaves being ready in the morning if he could put the armory out of action.

"Here's the thing. The armory has explosives as well as back up weapons and it's kept locked. I brought a padlock with me in case something like that happened. I can use it. If we can't get in neither can they without some effort."

"This is good enough, I think. You came prepared."

"But group members have their personal weapons on them at all times. Too many for me to disable one by one. So they'll be armed. No grenades, but rifles, handguns, blades."

Cascadia nodded. "I understand." She told him she would warn all the HOGs. Then she said that Shaylee and the slaves would be ready at dawn when the guard opened the door to their quarters. The male slaves would take him down and leave him locked in the slave quarters. The women would go to the cookhouse as usual. They would lower the panels over the screens so nobody could watch their movements. "They will set a grease fire while pretending to start breakfast. When that is done, they can all run for freedom."

"How are you alerting the Horde?"

"I have sent Hammer the woodpecker to everyone, even the pickers and the pot growers, to call them here. The fire will be everyone's sign that the slaves have been released and the slavers will follow soon."

"It's a good plan," Blake said. "Fire will lure everyone out of the cave. They won't know what is happening. It's safer for us to take them out here in the open than behind closed walls."

"You will be with Scorn in the morning?" the spirit asked. "She is your lust partner now?"

He didn't answer.

"Helen of Troy told me about women and wars. For centuries, human females have done what they must to stop male predators. I think it logical that a human male must do this, too, when the adversary is female."

"Yeah? Well I'm not so sure Shaylee would agree. I'm not proud of this deception."

"Pride cannot be your companion now. Whether or not Shaylee likes it, she will understand. You are the one who can stop Scorn. When you see the fire or smell the smoke, the slaves will be escaping. Scorn should not be allowed to run them down."

Cascadia could not see Blake but she heard his moan. "You're asking me to kill someone I know. She wasn't always Scorn. There was a time when Catherine was a person of worth. She mattered to me."

Cascadia needed help. In her head, Helen of Troy spoke to her, giving her the words for Blake. "It is the oldest story in all of mythology and history and time. A lover's betrayal. It is at the very creation of us all. You are not the first, Blake. But it is now your turn."

Blake exited the outhouse. He said to the approximate spot where he believed Cascadia must be, "Take my place in the human tragedy, huh? I live alone in the woods to avoid crises like this."

But he spoke only to himself. Cascadia was already gone.

* * *

By full dark, Nemesis and Achlys hovered in the sky above the camp, waiting. Cascadia had gone to Bird Woman to pick up Aiyana who griped all the way back about riding the bear. Silver Tip was glad to drop them in the forest near the compound clearing. He ambled away to find a vermin-infested tree stump to chew.

232

Jamie and Wren appeared soon after and hid with the spirit and the healer. Everyone stayed still but nearly shit themselves when Sas was suddenly just there. Wren made him snuff his blunt.

"It's not likely the guards have night goggles, but it's worth the precaution. Besides, they could smell the weed." Wren said.

"Why not night goggles?" Jamie asked.

"You've seen too much TV. They aren't funded by a first world military. They were just a bunch of assholes playing make believe until Scorn opened their eyes to slaving."

Cascadia told Jamie and Wren she had seen two perimeter guards as she was flying in, neither with special forces grade equipment other than their rifles. They should be neutralized before the slaves were released, but it must be done silently so the camp would not be alerted. "Come with me," she said.

She located the first guard and pointed him out to Jamie and Wren. Then she left them without a sound.

The guard seemed at ease. He was biting the cuticle on his thumbnail. Probably nothing ever happened out here. Maybe a cougar would pass by or an owl flap through. What could go wrong? He moved on to the other thumb. Then a whispery rustle caught his attention. When he looked up, a geisha stood before him.

He gasped and raised his gun. But he did not fire as the woman bowed, opened her silken kimono and touched her own naked nipples. She raised her arms to unpin her luxuriant mane of ebony hair. "I am at your command," the apparition said to him.

He gasped again, lowering the gun. He'd had fantasies about such a beauty who found him to be the most desirable of men. The strongest, the sexiest ... but of course that was a daydream. This woman couldn't be here. Had he been drinking? Smoking?

He gasped yet again when Jamie chambered a round next to his ear and whispered, "Not one sound, motherfucker. Not one." Wren took the guard's gun away, tied his hands and duct taped his mouth. Then Jamie and Wren drew him far back into the tree line and tied him to a massive log.

The next guard had a similar experience when he saw the cowgirl of his dreams in nothing but a fringed buckskin vest and, of course, boots. After he was tied to the same log as the first man, the HOGs returned to the spot they'd left Sas helping Aiyana arrange her herbs and weeds, probably hoping for a new kind of high.

"What appeared to those men, Cascadia? What fantasies did they see when they looked at you?" Wren asked in a controlled voice as they walked.

"I do not know, Wren," Cascadia replied. "But when I looked down at myself, I saw silk and then leather. I can feel the outfits and see them when the male is my target, but I don't know what they represent. I can only say humans have a wide range of taste in clothing."

"That's a rather handy defense system you have there," Jamie said, having never revealed what he saw in her.

"Yes. Unless they catch me. As one named Spider nearly did."

* * *

Just before dawn two pot growers and three pickers arrived, and Cascadia disappeared under her cloak of invisibility once again. Wren told the makeshift warriors to station themselves around the perimeter and wait for a bonfire. Survivalists and slaves would both appear after that. "Watch for yellow scarves. Those are the slaves. Let them go."

Cascadia left for the slave quonset. She whispered to Elpis who emerged from her acorn, assumed the size of a falcon, and perched on the spirit's forearm. Cascadia said, "It is up to you now, shape shifting goddess. You must help Shaylee convince the slaves to escape. They all need hope now."

Falcon-size was a perfect choice for swift flight but not for knot holes. Elpis said, "I fly high to the chink in the wall where I make myself small. A songbird I should think." She soared to the small screened window at the end of the quonset then settled on its frame as a canary. There she hopped along the frame until she found the tiny knot hole in the wood just below it. And there she cocked her bright yellow head to listen as Shaylee pleaded on the inside of the room.

* * *

Shaylee had cajoled the slaves for what seemed like hours. Only one agreed to follow her. Bonnie said, "We're not going to get a better chance than this. It's no good waiting. Besides, I'd rather die than stay here another night."

The rest were interested. They wanted to make a run for it. They discussed it with each other. They hemmed, they hawed. But in the end, Shaylee was greeted with a front of five shaking heads. "The danger is too high. We will fail."

That's when Elpis, cheery as Tweetie, pushed through the wall with an audible pop. She descended on a silken twist of brilliant yellow scarves. Shades of lemon, banana and daffodil glowed even in the dimness of the slave quarters. Each scarf was sprinkled with a layer of golden dust.

"I bring you a Rope of Hope!" said the fairy. "The unattainable is now gainable, the deniable now viable!" She gave the vine a flick of her wrist and the scarves separated. They floated onto the shoulders of each and every slave, Shaylee included.

It was as though the very room inhaled a breath of possibility. Wellbeing spread from lost soul to lost soul. Elpis giggled and grinned, her yellow feathers trembling in the air. "It's no longer unbelievable that escape is achievable."

Shaylee had never actually seen Elpis but her surprise was nothing compared to the slaves' reaction. As they wrapped their scarves around shoulders, head or neck, they gawked and gaped. Spines straightened and heads raised. They were touched with camaraderie and charged with optimism.

Of course they would escape! Of course it was worth the risk! While the slaves steeled themselves,

Elpis landed before Shaylee and assumed the size of a ten year old. The fairy first told her that Blake would lock the armory so the mission was a go. Then she lifted a small golden box and handed it to Shaylee to open. "Shield your eyes; it's quite a surprise."

Shaylee squinted and slowly opened the lid of the ornate container. Light beams shot out in the red, orange and blue hues of flame. She peeked into the box at a pellet shivering with such light. It was not hot but it was terrifying. She quickly shut the lid.

"Herein fire is stored, Shaylee Ward. A gift from the great god Prometheus to you. He has given humans fire before, but this is more. A concentrate for a blaze to raise a hotter faster alarm."

"What does it do?"

"It works like a charm this Essence of Inferno, don't you know. Release it into the hot cookhouse grease, then exit fast to avoid the blast. Take heed ...you will need great speed."

Shaylee pocketed the fire-in-a-box thinking when the time came to write her memoir, nobody would believe any of this. When she looked up, Elpis had shifted shape to a canary again and was just flitting back out the chink in the wall.

Shaylee turned to the six slaves, who were slapping backs and in general pumping each other up. Maybe they weren't equal to the Horde of Goodness but they certainly had taken hold of their own futures. They were ready for either flight or fight. She found it hard to settle them down, to explain the plan once more, and to await the morning light.

That went for herself as well.

237

* * *

Cascadia waited nearby, curled up with her bear. Elpis returned to her and sheltered in her acorn. The little goddess had done her part in giving the slaves hope.

There was no morning sunrise, more a lightening in the drizzle and gray. It was full dark and then it was not. Cascadia watched the slave guard emerge from the cave, scratch his ass, walk to the outhouse then down the slope to open the door to the slave quonset. He was unprepared for three men in yellow headgear, all leaping upon him. He flailed and cursed but they dragged him into the quonset and Cascadia had no vision of what they did to him in there. But he did not come back out.

Instead, the women led by Shaylee emerged and walked quickly to the cookhouse as usual, raising no alarm from any other survivalist who might be an early riser.

Cascadia saw the wooden panels come down over the screens. She saw the glow of the light when the fire was lit. She smelled hot cooking grease. Then she heard Shaylee yell, "All of you. Run for the woods." Three women took off, yellow scarves streaming behind them. Shaylee came out, removed a box from her pocket, threw it into the cookhouse, then ran at a speed even Cascadia could never match.

One second. Two. The building disintegrated in a massive fireball.

* * *

The coydog Shadow had watched all day from the woods. She'd seen Shaylee kill the man. She'd seen the fairy enter the slave quarters. She'd seen Cascadia curl up with the bear. And she'd seen her master Blake enter the cave with the woman she did not like. At the blast of the fire, she knew exactly what to do.

She raced to Blue, terrifying the other five horses and mules in the corral. Blue backed against the gate giving it a mighty push with his massive butt. It cracked and tumbled like it was made of matchsticks. Growling and snapping, Shadow scared the other hayburners through the new opening. They thundered off with Blue nipping them from behind.

* * *

Blake watched Scorn's lovely face as she drifted into a soft sleep. He touched her cheek and pulled the blanket up to her shoulders. He put on his pants but didn't bother with a shirt, leaving to place the padlock on the armory door. She'd never know he'd been gone.

But that was not to be. Scorn followed him and watched his betrayal as he clicked the lock home. "I knew it was too good to be true," she said with contempt that vibrated in the air. "I knew you were treacherous, you double-dealing bastard."

Blake turned to her. "The lock is already on the door. I have no idea of the combination. It can't be undone."

"You've lied to me, used me. That slave of yours killed my crew boss and you planned it. She's no slave at all. Just another of your fucks. You're both here to destroy this place."

She raised a gun. He saw it tremble in her hand. She was enraged, the lines of her face distorted with it. He did not want to kill her, but he did not want to die.

Flame from the cookhouse burst into the sky. Scorn faltered but not enough for Blake to take the gun. She was far too capable a fighter for that.

He stepped closer and held out a hand. "Come with me, Catherine. End this now. Let the slaves go free. No one needs to die."

"No Blake. One of us definitely does need to die." She fired. Once, twice. Blake fell. As his blood mingled with earth, Scorn wrenched a key from his pants pocket, then ran screaming for her troops to take the field.

Blake lived maybe a moment or two. Long enough to whisper a good-bye to Shaylee that nobody heard. By the time Shadow found him, her beloved master was dead. The coydog whimpered, licked his hand. Then she began to howl and did not stop.

CHAPTER NINETEEN

Confusion. Yelling. Gun fire. The howl of an animal in pain. The next half hour was madness. Shaylee saw men and women exit the cave brandishing rifles, gaping at the fire, hammering on a locked armory door, avoiding terrified livestock thundering across the clearing. A topaz yellow scarf snagged on a bush half way down the slope waved although rain was slowly weighing it down. A slave had either lost it or her life, maybe both.

Shaylee saw signs of the Horde of Goodness hard at work. Pot growers were pulling slaves into the woods as pickers swung machetes at the first survivalists to reach the bottom of the hill. Aiyana was at the side of a fallen soldier while Achlys awaited her chance to finish him off. Jamie and Wren both trapped slavers who were heading AWOL. Wren used a rifle butt and Jamie his fists. Two men were down and out.

In the midst of it all, Shaylee couldn't find Blake. Where the hell was he? She had no time to search because she saw Scorn, standing in the center of the field, urging her troops on. Blake had failed to stop her.

Maybe he didn't want to. Maybe he couldn't't.

Shaylee looked for a weapon, found no gun but saw a combat knife next to a fallen slaver. She grabbed it up and stalked her prey.

* * *

Aiyana bent over one of the pickers. A bullet had found its way through the young girl's jaw and out a cheek. The victim's hot blood covered Aiyana's hands as the healer tried to apply a yarrow and cayenne poultice to the wound.

"She will bleed out," scoffed Achlys. "You will fail to save her."

Misery's fetid breath behind the healer's head made Aiyanna fear she would retch.

"I will take her now." Achlys spread her arms wide and beseeched the Death Mist to burst free from her gnarled fingertips.

Aiyana turned, savage as a rabid dog. "You'll do no such thing," she commanded, standing tall between the goddess and the wounded warrior. She pushed Achlys hard in the chest, knocking her back and down. But the Death Mist had released. It hit Aiyana full in the face and clung like a veil, clouding her vision. The healer clutched her throat unable to breath. She had just enough air to gasp Cascadia's name. Then she fell like a rag doll next to the young picker on the ground.

Achlys gloated at her triumph, wallowing in pride at the size of her prize. She had taken down a healer! She was undefeatable! "I can afford to let you live," she said in disdain to the wounded picker. "Or maybe you'll die. If not, the scar with disfigure you for the rest of your life."

* * *

Cascadia found Blake and wanted to save Shaylee the harrowing sight. There would be time for that torment when the skirmish was won. She was placing the broken body on Silver Tip's broad back when she heard Aiyana call her name. The spirit ordered the bear to fly his precious cargo carefully back to Bird Woman then she dashed to the battlefield where Aiyana now lay still.

Aiyana! One of the two humans she loved. *Aiyana!* How desperately emotions could hurt.

Cascadia lunged at the gloating Keeper of the Death Mist. She clutched the bent figure by the throat, quelling her insane laughter. Cascadia removed her Bowie knife from its white leather sheath. It gleamed with deadly intent. Achlys struggled like an animal in a live trap, but it did not faze the angry spirit. Cascadia hissed, "I will kill you slowly, goddess."

"Stop!" Elpis left her acorn and grew to the size of a condor. "Fail you will. A spirit cannot a goddess kill."

Cascadia felt woozy with her despair. "She must be punished."

"'Tis true and good news for you! A goddess can kill a goddess." Elpis struck with such force that her talons ripped a great hole in the narrow chest of Achlys.

The Catalyst made a grab for a fluffy yellow wing but Elpis twisted away, dodging whatever mist the goddess might have left to spread. She was making another pass that would finish the affair when the griffins blocked her way.

"Elpis! This is no way for a fairy to fight!" Nemesis was the very portrait of consternation. She ordered the griffins to pick up the moaning heap that was Achlys. They cawed in protest but finally did as they were told, each grabbing a piece of the hoary cloak in its beak.

"Join me in my chariot, my feathered friend. I must consider what has happened here then judge the consequences." The Punisher sighed. "I cannot really kill Achlys or I'll never know if she can be reformed."

"This 'tis true, too. So I will come with you." Elpis shape shifted to the size of a squirrel and perched on the Punisher's shoulder. As the chariot lifted off, she called to Cascadia. "Hope may not always win. Then again, it alone can vanquish anguish, conquer gloom and doom. Never forget, my pet."

Nemesis, Achlys and Elpis flew away leaving behind a very dispirited spirit. Cascadia bent down and cradled the body of her friend. Once again that mysterious water appeared from her eyes and ran down her cheeks. Surely this ache she felt was a canyon too deep to ever fill.

Then, cradled to the spirit's chest, Aiyana said in a muffled voice, "I'm not dead. But I may be if you drown me."

* * *

Shaylee did not have a magic Web of Revenge to capture Scorn. Nor did she have invisibility on her side. She was not a prize fighter so she wouldn't start a fist fight. She couldn't swing a lasso and hog tie the woman. She could stab with a knife but without the kind of accuracy to be sure of cutting a major blood vessel or piercing the spine until it was paralyzed.

Still, Shaylee felt ruthless. And she was crazy strong from all the years of logging. Few women were her physical match. Scorn had stolen people's freedom, she'd stolen safety from everyone in the forest, and now she may have stolen Blake from Shaylee. Scorn was going to pay.

Apparently Scorn had a different rulebook. She not only saw Shaylee charging, she watched her come. As Shaylee drew close, Scorn fired her handgun. To both their amazement, Shaylee kept on coming.

She knew she'd been hit somewhere in the flesh of her thigh. But she felt nothing. Shock blocked it, maybe. She'd heard of people being unaware of wounds until danger passed. If she could irritate Scorn into talking, maybe she could get closer still.

"Blake doesn't want you, Scorn. You're such a skank."

Scorn looked at her contemptuously but otherwise didn't react as Shaylee expected with curses of her own. Instead, she laughed. And then Scorn said, "You don't even know he's dead, do you? I killed the bastard."

That was the wound Shaylee felt. Searing pain. Blinding rage. She exploded in lethal fury lunging as Scorn was raising the gun again. It was the kind of leap she made from log to log almost every day. It took Shaylee too close for a shot from an extended arm, a target too hard to hit. She slammed into Scorn,

245

grabbed her shoulder with one hand and held her tight around the neck as she sunk the knife into soft tissue somewhere below. Near the stomach maybe or intestines.

But then Shaylee stumbled. The wound to her thigh was catching up with her. Scorn stumbled as well. They supported each other in an awkward embrace, as they executed a slow motion ballet like dying swans.

Lying on the ground, as the world began to spin, Shaylee heard someone yell, "We have to get out of here." Just before black out she saw a man pull Scorn up and help her limp away.

* * *

The fight was nearly over. Most of the slavers were wounded or long gone. An eerie silence descended as the last guns fired and knives slashed. It would be some time before birds would return to add music to this part of the forest.

Then an unexpected noise arrived. It was the sound of motion in the trees, but not wind because it rustled from all directions. And then they appeared. By the dozen. By the hundreds. Sasquatches. All large and silent as they became visible, surrounding the field of battle.

The slavers stopped the last of their fighting. Many felt terror of these mythical monsters. If they could still run, they did, escaping into the woods. As for the Horde of Goodness, they dropped their jaws in wonder.

Jamie had applied a tourniquet to Shaylee's leg under the guidance of a very weakened Aiyana. Wren and Cascadia were on guard. Only the appearance of hundreds of silent creatures broke into Shaylee's thoughts of Blake.

"Sas?" she called while the beasts began to tear the survivalist camp apart at a speed that rivaled light.

"You bellowed, Mama?" he said, truckin' toward her. "You do that a lot."

"Who ... what?"

"You mean, all these 'squatches? This is my family, dudes and dudettes. We're always around, just too fast for you humans to see very often."

"What's going on?" Jamie asked.

"Gotta destroy this camp. Leave no trace. We don't want more of you coming to the woods. Not safe for too many people to get too close. You're a damn bloodthirsty group, you know."

Shaylee looked around at the field. Everywhere work crews of sasquatches were picking up bodies, disassembling buildings, busting up the armory, carrying everything away. The slaves were gone other than Bonnie who was with the HOGs. It looked like Jamie had given her his jacket to wear in the chill damp.

"If it was up to us, you'd all get the hell out." Sas shrugged. "Even you so called do-gooders. Although I gotta say, it's been real." Then he was gone along with the camp and the rest of his clan. Their existence was merely a myth once more.

"Okay then," said Shaylee. Looking around, she could finally ask her real question. "Scorn said Blake was dead. He's not here now. Tell me."

Wren answered. "As best we can piece together, she shot him, Shaylee. Cascadia found his body just outside the armory. And that's where Scorn was when she began shouting for her troops."

"Silver Tip carried Blake to Bird Woman. Blue will take you there now." Cascadia called the horse from the treeline. Shadow was close to his side and came directly to Shaylee. For the first time, the coydog allowed herself to be touched.

"Looks like she's choosing you now, Shaylee. Blake's Shadow will be with you." Jamie looked embarrassed by his loving statement as he lifted Shaylee aboard Blue. But she hugged him. After he'd placed Aiyana on the horse behind Shaylee, they began the long walk home.

* * *

The women of Bird Woman welcomed the HOGs and were especially joyful to see Bonnie. They fed them, cared for them. They had cleansed Blake's body and covered his broken chest with a clean white t-shirt. It was the best they could do. Then they had placed him in a room at the main house, allowing a man inside for the first time. They wanted Shaylee to have time with the body if she needed it to say good-bye. But she didn't. She wanted her last image of Blake to be the way he was in life.

The HOGs talked around the campfire as dusk dissolved into night. Cascadia joined and sat close to Aiyana who was weak but would hopefully recover soon. The healer told them how she had defeated the Death Mist. "I knew shit could happen, that Achlys was not to be trusted especially with me. So I made a solution from the sorcerer's berries of deadly nightshade. It's a form of atropine that is an antidote to mists like nerve agents, chemical warfare, pesticides. I thought the Death Mist must work like them. It tries to stop the heart but this antidote regulates it. I gulped it down just before the battle began. Glad it worked."

Wren told the group she and Aiyana had talked. The healer would stay at Bird Woman while she recovered. "And I hope she'll stay after that. We could use medical help around here."

"You would not be alone anymore, Aiyana. This would be good," Cascadia said with a smile.

Shaylee realized how at home the spirit was becoming with humans. *One of us.* She was not the stranger in a strange land she had once been. It might be time to teach her to read so she could choose her own t-shirts.

Jamie and Wren said the pickers and growers had returned to their own routines. The pickers had not found their group member among the slaves who had escaped, but the pot growers did. Bonnie, still wearing Jamie's jacket and tucked next to him said she remembered the picker's slave as the man they had seen eviscerated. She said he'd been very brave and a fine man. The pickers had said they'd return the rest of the freed slaves to the homeless camp or out of the woods altogether. Some of the survivalists might still be loose in the woods and represent a danger to them. But they figured most had high-tailed it out of the forest long ago.

The one missing was Scorn. Shaylee knew she had wounded the woman, but not how badly. They needed to find her if she was still alive. She might start another camp or plan some other sort of evil. And besides. Shaylee was not sure the despair she felt over the loss of Blake would die until Scorn did.

"Will you and Silver Tip search for her, Cascadia?" Wren asked.

"Speaking of Silver Tip, where is he? Jamie asked. "I didn't see him with Blue when I took him some oats."

Cascadia pointed into the night. "He is there."

They were startled by the sound of an airplane engine. Small, close. It must be Blake's old Cessna, the one he'd used to help the compound's women migrate to new homes.

They ran toward the airstrip. There were no lights but the sky had cleared and a fat moon washed the meadow in blue. The little plane bounced and gained speed enough to take off.

"Who is it?" Bonnie yelled.

Cascadia was the one who knew. "It is Scorn. But she will not get away."

"Sure looks like she is ... must have taken the ignition key from Blake," Wren guessed.

"A human in a machine cannot outfly a bear."

They couldn't see Silver Tip in the dark. But they saw the plane suddenly tilt. A wing bounced and a piece of undercarriage blew away. As the plane fell from the sky, they heard a mighty ursine roar of delight.

"I will have to pick berries for him for a week," Cascadia said as the wreckage hit the ground.

* * *

They made sure the flames from the plane crash was out. No one, not even Scorn, could have escaped that flame-thrower of an ending. They went back to their campfire for a last drink of coffee with or without the brandy that Bird Woman made from wild blackberries.

Shaylee listened to the chatter about who had been bravest on the battlefield and how surprising the sasquatches had been and whether the homeless camp might be brought under the protection of Bird Woman, too. But in time, she knew it was Blake she needed to talk with. She wandered away. Shadow tagged along. The coydog had decided that her shyness with one human had led to bad things. She wasn't going to make that mistake with this human.

Shaylee wanted to tell Blake that she had never really doubted him. Not really. She thanked him for loving her with all her insecurities. He'd helped her discover that she had value. At heart, she knew he had been as broken as she was, probably more so. Blake would have always been as much a creature of the woods as the Sasquatch. He was lost to his own kind. L,,,As she thought these things, First Female spoke to her, a gentle music in her head. "He was one of my better creations."

"Yes, he was."

"But it was time for you to part. You must move on."

"I know. But it happened so fast. I can't catch my breath. And I'm so afraid."

"Of course you are. But you must accept you are a human leader. You can do more than hide in the forest. Civilization has need of you. Blake knew that."

"He made me whole."

"He helped you, yes. But you're the one who conquered your past."

"I don't know what lies ahead for me now."

"Not important. It's only important that I do. And I promise it will be astounding."

CHAPTER TWENTY

Old Man Above loved to putter. He demoted planets and promoted moons, drew up plans for a thunderbird so big it could not get off the ground, improved on honey-wine by adding forbidden fruit. He was not above making the centaurs race the satyrs merely so he could place a bet he was sure to win.

First Female had little patience for such tinkering, considering it wasted time. Old Man Above had come to hate the phrase 'what are you up to now?'

"What are you up to now?" First Female asked, knowing he'd be late for Cascadia's presentation if she didn't nudge him a time or two.

"Nothing, my shining treasure. Just hoping you'd happen along."

"It is time for Cascadia to issue her final report on the problem with people."

"Ingrates. I say we start over. Annihilate them with volcano, crush them with avalanche, bury them with earthquake, drown them with deluge, burn them with wildfire."

She waited for him to wind down. "If we start over, you may just make the same mistake all over again."

"Me? Who says I made a mistake?"

"Well you are a little lax when it comes to creation, my dear. Besides, there is much decency in them as is. Why throw out the good with the bad? At least let us listen to what Cascadia has to say."

"I'm not good at listening."

"No, you are not."

"This leads to criticism of me. I just knew it would."

"Perhaps the mistake is not yours but mine."

Old Man Above knew a trap when he heard it. "But you are perfect, my luscious sweet. I am merely nearly so."

Both parties appeased, they readied themselves to greet the spirit.

* * *

Cascadia arrived at the Chamber of Mythology. She was now so versed in human emotion she knew that what she was feeling was nervous. Her stomach danced and her legs trembled.

This was no-spirits-land, exclusive territory of gods and goddesses. She was the very first spirit ever allowed within these hallowed walls, and she was very much aware of what an honor had been bestowed. Cascadia would have felt better with Shaylee by her side, but no living human would ever enter. It was rare enough that one of the greats from the Tree of Human History made an appearance.

At least she had Silver Tip. She touched him for reassurance. She had bathed him in her favorite pool, then thoroughly groomed the burrs and twigs from his fur. She'd dressed in her most formal shorts and a little black *Puttin' on the Ritz* t-shirt.

Cascadia had never before actually seen Old Man Above and First Female. And she didn't see them now. She'd been told that to view them was to be sucked into a black hole where one's brain would turn to porridge. Now two glowing auras undulated before her like the wavering color sheets of the Northern Lights. One aura was all the hues on earth, the other decidedly solemn in deep purples and black. One was welcoming, the other a gathering storm.

Three other Presences graced the room and their nearness cheered her. Here were the goddesses, her mentors. Helen of Troy posed on a golden throne, Nemesis on a bed of nails, and Elpis on a perch. Lust, Outrage and Hope. These three had helped her understand human nature and intuit other emotions as well. She was no longer the naive little lump of ooze she'd been before First Female sang her Creation Song.

"Welcome, Spirit." First Female's voice came to Cascadia as a breathy song. "You may speak."

She began in a breathy voice herself but gained strength as she continued. "First Female and Old Man Above. You created me to walk among the humans and discover what is wrong with them. What I discovered was how much good they have, what a credit to you they are. They are awesome creations, rich in love and joy."

"This is boring," Old Man Above whispered to First Female. She shushed him.

Cascadia moved quickly to the grittier bits. "But it is true that sometimes they hurt each other. This happens when their ugly emotions get the best of their good. Because every good emotion has its opposite. One can slide up or down a scale to eclipse the other. Love has hate. Openheartedness has envy. Generosity has greed. It is most complex."

"We know this, Spirit. It's the *why* we seek." Old Man Above's voice sounded to her like far away thunder.

"What you may not realize is that emotion is only half of a person. The other half is logic. You built them far smarter than your other creations. They can figure things out, create, reason. But when logic is impaired, emotions turn base. It is a juggling act. Emotion must stay in balance with itself. Logic and emotion must stay in balance with each other."

Cascadia heard Helen of Troy whisper to Nemesis, "That's our girl!"

Nemesis frowned her to silence.

"There are four things you can do. Number one, the human healer Aiyana told me it would not hurt for you to add a dash more oxytocin to the ooze you use for their creation. It will help them stop arguing."

"We have used this trust hormone in animals for hundreds of millions of years. Even in fish." First Female's singing changed to a higher key.

"Aiyana says if you ramp it up a bit, humans will be kinder, show more compassion. The more empathy they have, the less evil they will do. She says while you're at it, could you please add some to wolverines as well."

Old Man Above rumbled. "Fine, fine. So we destroy the people we have now and replace them with a new improved model. Problem solved. Are we done?"

"Not so hasty, my love. The spirit has just begun."

"Number Two," Cascadia continued. "Humans must always have hope. Despair drains it away and their logic is impaired. I suggest you give Elpis a higher seat in the Chamber of Mythology. Treat her with more importance. Do not lose her in small spaces." From the corner of her eye, Cascadia saw Elpis brighten even more than normal.

"Number Three. Humans need a little more guidance from above. Sometimes you are ... ah ... cryptic. Difficult to understand."

A great growl from the darker aura. "We make ourselves perfectly clear."

"If you speak more than smite, humans will understand you better." Cascadia rushed to move forward. "And Four. The humans who exist now have great worth with just a little guidance. I propose a council to monitor their behavior. Include on the council these fine goddesses, of course. I also propose my familiar, Shaylee Ward to speak for humanity. Let them judge the day to day. And if it appears that badness is overtaking good, then allow the Punisher to do what she is born to do." Now even Nemesis looked pleased.

There was a pause while rumble and song became one in an unworldly symphony that a mere spirit could not comprehend. Not even Helen, Nemesis or Elpis could understand this language of the highest of the high.

When their discussion was complete, First Female announced, "Your suggestions shall be implemented. You have done well, Cascadia. And you shall be rewarded by the removal of tools you've been given."

Cascadia felt confused. Shouldn't she be given more? But she held her tongue. Never look a gift goddess in the mouth.

From the back of beyond, Antigonus the Gladiator appeared. His battered old face beamed at her and Cascadia delightedly gave him a hug. He said, "I come for the Web of Revenge, little one. You will need it no more." He removed it gently where it coiled on her shoulder, kissed her cheek and then was gone.

Jim Bowie appeared in his place, grabbed her up and held her close in a very different kind of hug. He removed the knife from its white leather sheath. "I must go back to the Alamo, my unforgettable Miss Cassie. I will make use of this there. God's teeth how I loved you."

Helen left her throne and handed her a goblet, telling her to drink. As she did, the Goddess of Lust said, "This is the antidote to my elixir. You have no need to be a man's fantasy anymore. Men will see you as you are or not at all." She locked arms with Jim Bowie and the two left together.

The Ring of Gyges was next. Nemesis took it from her. "You are no longer required to judge the integrity of men. I will save it for the next time such a need arises. Now I must go locate those silly griffins." She touched Cascadia's forehead and the memory of the magic words which activated the ring disappeared from Cascadia's brain. Then the Daughter of Night was gone.

Elpis fluttered near. "I must take my acorn back in that it's my home away from home, but here is a feather of hope for you to wear wherever you may roam." The exchange was made and the fairy flew away.

Cascadia suddenly knew what was next. Her heart pounded and then began to break. She gasped, "Silver Tip!"

"He is a great bear, spirit, but an elderly one. He will be returned to a meadow full of honey, a pool bursting with fish, a lovely warm den, and a beautiful brown bear to keep him company. He will no longer fly. But he will be happy in the way bears are meant to be. His life will be long and sweet."

Cascadia knew it was for the best and after a final scratch to a teddy bear ear, she watched him fade away. But so did her sorrow. She felt only joy for him. Or was it the wind that suddenly blew in the chamber? She shivered a shiver of pleasure.

"Invisibility you shall keep, as our thanks to you, spirit. With it you may wander safe and free with Dogoda, the spirit of the West Wind."

Cascadia's delight swelled. From the day First Female sang her creation song, Cascadia had found Dogoda irresistible. They swirled and danced in the air, open to every touch. He enthralled her, she cherished him. Yet every year he had to leave as the season gave way to another.

"You will remain with him, although you may visit Shaylee from time to time. And if we need help with humans again, then you must return. Is that acceptable?"

"Ah, yes. So very yes." With that she felt the arms of the West Wind pick her up and carry her away.

"Well that settles that," said Old Man Above, glad they were alone in the chamber. He could get back to doing very little. "We have a plan and your little spirit is happy."

"It has ended well, I think." First Female loved a happy ending. "A brand new future starts today."

"Without a doubt, my cherished darling. Now what's for dinner?"

THE END

Author's Acknowledgments

As always, I am indebted to my sister and researcher, Donna Whichello. For factual content in *The Slightly Altered History of Cascadia*, I thank many experts, librarians, gods and goddesses, as well as websites.

I am sincerely grateful to Heidi Hansen, Jon Eekhoff, Melee Vander Veldt, Beth Pratt and Kimberly Minard, all members of my excellent critique group. To the readers of my stories, you are my cheerleaders when I am flagging.

I am also very grateful to live in Cascadia. The Pacific Northwest is a magical place for its wildness, remarkable beauty and the mysteries it holds close deep in the mountains and woods.

About the Author

Linda B. Myers won her first creative contest in the sixth grade for her *Clean Up Fix Up Paint Up* poster. After a Chicago marketing career, she traded in her snow boots for rain boots and moved to the Pacific Northwest with her Maltese Dotty. You can visit with Linda on her blog at www.lindabmyers.com

Look for other novels
by Linda B. Myers

Available at www.amazon.com

Lessons of Evil
Oregon, 1989. Psychologist Laura Covington joins a community mental health department. One of her new clients is so traumatized he suffers Multiple Personality Disorder. Through him, Laura discovers a desert cult and the vicious psychopath who commands it. Laura has unleashed dangerous secrets and now, she must decide how far she is willing to go to protect everything she loves. This is psychological suspense geared to keep you guessing as it builds toward its unpredictable conclusion.

A Time of Secrets: A Big Island Mystery
Life is uncomplicated in a Big Island village until Maile Palea, an 8-year-old girl, disappears. Twelve years later she is still missing. This is the story of her sister and brother who never give up trying to find her and cannot heal until they do, of a village that no longer feels safe from a changing world, and of a perpetrator who discovers what disastrous things happen when you keep secrets too long. A perfect read for fans of edgy suspense and hot Hawaiian nights.

Fun House Chronicles

Self-reliant Lily Gilbert enters a nursing home ready to kick administrative butt until the chill realities of the place nearly flatten her. She calls it the Fun House for the scary sights and sounds that await her there. Soon other quirky residents and caregivers draw Lily and her daughter in as they grapple with their own challenges. Lily discovers each stage of life can be its own adventure with more than a few surprises along the way. The characters in the Bear Jacob Mystery series made their first appearance in *Fun House Chronicles*.

The Bear Jacobs Mystery Series

Meet retired PI Bear Jacobs, his eWatson Lily Gilbert, and the rest of the quirky residents at Latin's Ranch Adult Family Home in the Pacific Northwest. Yes, they are infirm. Yes, they gripe. But all the while, they solve crimes, dodge bullets and stand tall on their canes, walkers and wheels. Enjoy this whole series of cozies
with bite.

Book One. *Bear in Mind*

The Latin's Ranch residents investigate the case of Charlie's missing wife. Is she a heart breaking bitch who abandoned her hubby? Or is a madman attacking older women? When others in the community disappear, Bear and his gang follow a dangerous and twisted trail to a surprising conclusion.

Book Two. *Hard to Bear*

A vicious crew is producing old-fashioned snuff films with a violent new twist: custom-order murder for sale. The Latin's Ranch gang takes on the villains behind this updated evil, coming under danger themselves. Bear joins forces with an avenging mob family, a special forces soldier tormented by PTSD, and a pack of mad dogs on the loose in the Pacific Northwest woods.

Novella One. *Bear Claus*

PI Bear Jacobs is mired down with seasonal depression until his e-Watson, Lily, finds him a mystery to solve. The trail is both fun and fearsome as it leads from theft in the My Fair Pair lingerie shop through a local casino to a dangerous solution in the Northwest Forest. Bear
Claus is a Christmas novella.

Book Three. *Bear at Sea*

When Eunice wins the Arctic Angel Award, the Latin's Ranch gang cruises to Alaska to pick up her prize. But high life on shipboard is dashed by low life murderers and thieves. One of their aides is struck down, and Eunice's life is threatened not once but twice. The gang takes action, endangering themselves to solve the case of the short-tailed albatross.

Made in the USA
Lexington, KY
03 October 2017